Dedalus Europea
General Editor: Mi

The Class

Hermann Ungar

The Class

Translated by Mike Mitchell

Dedalus

LOTTERY FUNDED

Published in the UK by Dedalus Ltd,
Langford Lodge, St Judith's Lane, Sawtry, Cambs, PE28 5XE
email: DedalusLimited@compuserve.com
www.dedalusbooks.com

ISBN 1 903517 19 2

Dedalus is distributed in the United States by SCB Distributors,
15608 South New Century Drive, Gardena, California 90248
email: info@scbdistributors.com   web site: www.scbdistributors.com

Dedalus is distributed in Australia & New Zealand by Peribo Pty Ltd,
58 Beaumont Road, Mount Kuring-gai N.S.W. 2080
email: peribo@bigpond.com

Dedalus is distributed in Canada by Marginal Distribution,
695, Westney Road South, Suite 14 Ajax, Ontario, L16 6M9
email: marginal@marginalbook.com   web site: www.marginalbook.com

Publishing History
First published in German in 1927
First published by Dedalus in 2004

Translation copyright©Mike Mitchell 2003.

The right of Mike Mitchell to be identified as the translator of this work has been
asserted by him in accordance with the Copyright, Designs and Patent Act, 1988.

Printed in Finland by WS Bookwell
Typeset by RefineCatch Ltd, Bungay, Suffolk

A C.I.P. listing for this book is available on request.

THE AUTHOR

Hermann Ungar (1893–1929) was a German-speaking Jew from Moravia who was active as a writer in Berlin and Prague in the 1920s. Critics spoke of him in the same breath as Kafka, and he was feted in France after the publication of the translation of *The Maimed* in 1928.

After the war he was largely forgotten in Germany, despite praise from individual writers, but the reissue of the French translation in 1987 was again greeted with enthusiastic reviews: 'Hermann Ungar is a great writer, unique . . . No history of literature should ignore his works.'

THE TRANSLATOR

Mike Mitchell is one of Dedalus's editorial directors and is responsible for the Dedalus translation programme. His publications include *The Dedalus Book of Austrian Fantasy 1890–2000* and *Austria* in the *World Bibliographical Series*.

Mike Mitchell's translations include all the novels of Gustav Meyrink, three by Herbert Rosendorfer, three by Grimmelshausen and the *Plays and Poems of Oskar Kokoschka*.

His translation of Rosendorfer's *Letters Back to Ancient China* won the 1998 Schlegel-Tieck German Translation Prize.

Foreword

After the publication of his second novel, *The Class*, in 1927, the main Viennese newspaper, the *Neue Freie Presse*, called Hermann Ungar 'the most important writer of the decade'. And that in one of the most hectic decades in German literature when, among the younger generation, figures such as Franz Werfel, Joseph Roth, Ernst Toller, Alfred Döblin, Bertolt Brecht, Leo Perutz, Paul Kornfeld, Ernst Weiss, Egon Erwin Kisch were active. Unlike another German-speaking Jewish writer from the region that was to become Czechoslovakia, Franz Kafka, with whom his name is often linked, Ungar was almost completely forgotten in Germany after the Second World War. In France, however, the issue of translations of his two novels and a volume with two short stories in 1987–88 (the stories and *The Maimed* had already appeared in France in the 1920s) was greeted with enthusiastic reviews and the recognition not only of his importance in the context of German literature between the wars, but of the abiding power of his portrayal of a world in which all the figures seem to be cripples: physical, psychological, emotional and moral cripples.

One critic, Vincent Ostria, declared that the excesses of punk musicians such as Sid Vicious looked 'small beer' compared to the extremes possible in literature as demonstrated by Ungar's novels. Both French and German critics have insisted on seeing in his characters, in which full humanity has been reduced to fear and hatred – often the hatred of their own selves – an adumbration of figures which in 1933 would 'step out of literary fiction and into reality'.

Hermann Ungar was born in 1893 in the Moravian town of Boskovice, into a wealthy, cultured Jewish family. His father owned a distillery and was mayor of the Jewish community, whose presence in the town went back to the 11th century. Boskovice was entirely Czech-speaking, but the Jewish community – until the end of the First World War the two parts of the town were separate – spoke German. Ungar grew up speaking both languages, but his education at high school and university was at German institutions.

The routine anti-semitism of some of his German fellow pupils in the high school in Brünn/Brno awakened an interest in Judaism and the Jewish religion, to which he had been largely indifferent until then. He decided to study Hebrew and Arabic in Berlin and joined the Jewish student corporation modelled on the German duelling fraternities, acting as its president in 1914, although by then he had transferred from Semitic languages to Law.

As with many other artists and writers, the war was an experience which fundamentally changed his outlook. He volunteered in 1914 and served for three years in the artillery before being seriously wounded and invalided out. He resumed his studies, completing his law degree at the (German) University of Prague in 1918. But this was a different Ungar. He abandoned the student fraternities, with their duels and colours, and renounced Zionism, which seemed to him in danger of becoming a new kind of nationalism.

He also seems to have thrown away or destroyed all his early writings, plays full of passion, violence and intrigue. It had always been Ungar's ambition to be a writer and for a short while he worked in the theatre in Eger/Egra, hoping it would be a milieu conducive to writing, but after a short time took a position in a bank. This led to work for the Czech Export Agency in Berlin and finally, in 1922, a post as commercial attaché at the Czech embassy there. Though the work was not particularly congenial to him, the Czech foreign ministry treated him generously, apparently pleased to encourage a man making a name for himself in German literature. (A press attaché at the embassy was another Czech-German writer, Camill Hoffmann.) In 1928 he was moved to the foreign ministry in Prague; on 10 October 1929 he resigned from his post; on 28 October he died of peritonitis after an appendix operation.

The works he wrote around the end of the war did not reach the public: a novel has disappeared and a play called *Krieg* (War) was not published until 1990. Two stories, gathered together under the title *Knaben und Mörder* (Boys and Murderers), appeared in 1920. *The Maimed* was published in 1923, to a reaction of horrified admiration, and his second novel, *The Class* in 1927. In 1928 his play *Der rote General* (The Red General) was performed with great success in Berlin. The central figure is a Jewish general who is abandoned by the Communists, once he is no longer needed, and executed by the White Russians. Some saw it as a portrait of Trotsky, which Ungar denied. A second play, a comedy called *Die Gartenlaube* (The Arbour),had its premiere six weeks after his death.

The main character of *The Class*, Josef Blau, is a schoolteacher who comes from a poor background, but teaches at a high school in a wealthy part of the town. Faced with a class of well-dressed, well-groomed pupils, he feels insecure. He is convinced they despise him and the rigid discipline he imposes on them is designed to prevent what he assumes is the contempt they feel for him from breaking out in 'rebellion'. Just as Polzer, the hero of *The Maimed*, feels that 'Once the order had been disrupted, ever increasing chaos was bound to follow,' so Blau 'fought with all the means at his disposal to maintain discipline. Once it was relaxed, everything was lost.'

But Blau's rigidity is not merely a reflection of his social insecurity. It goes much deeper than that and informs his whole existence, public, private and personal. He believes our lives – his especially – are inextricably interwoven with others' and subject to a fate which can be brought down on us by the slightest act: a movement, a word, even just breathing. His whole life is little more than an attempt to ward off, or at least delay what he sees as the inevitable. Everything he does may have consequences, for himself or for those around him, and therefore he feels everything he does involves him in guilt.

This attitude seems to be confirmed when the one positive action he takes leads to tragedy. He waits outside a brothel he has been told the pupil whom he regards as his chief enemy visits. He sees two pupils there and goes away believing he now has them under his control. For a short while he is transformed from the timid mouse into a masterful male. But one of the two boys commits suicide as a result of having been seen at the brothel, plunging Blau back into self-recrimination which erupts physically in a haemorrhage, a hereditary weakness.

Unlike *The Maimed*, *The Class* has a happy, or at least a conciliatory ending. Blau is not cured of his belief that he is inextricably involved in the fates of those around him, but when he is put, by a concatenation of ugly circumstances, in a position to help another pupil who is contemplating suicide, he at least sees that the involvement can also lead to good.

The theme of the schoolboy suicide is one that was surprisingly common, one might even call it a fashion, in the German literature of the late nineteenth and early twentieth century. Two of the early treatments of the theme are Emil Strauß's *Freund Hein* (The Grim Reaper, 1902) and Hermann Hesse's *Unterm Rad* (The Prodigy, 1906), and almost contemporary with *The Class* is Friedrich Torberg's *Der Schüler Gerber hat absolviert* (Gerber Finishes School, 1930); the best-known example internationally is Frank Wedekind's play *Frühlings Erwachen* (Spring Awakening, 1891).

In these other works the emphasis is generally social and psychological. The tragedies resulting from intolerable pressures exerted by the school system and parental expectations reflect on the authoritarian nature of society. *The Class*, however, focuses on the authority figure, not on the victim. In this it resembles another famous German novel, Heinrich Mann's *Professor Unrat* (1905), best known as the source of the film *The Blue Angel*. But whereas Mann's tyrant is the vehicle for a biting satire on the values of Wilhelmine Germany, Ungar's reflects an existential *angst* in which the social background is merely one contributory factor among many.

Another contributory factor is Blau's old school-friend, the bizarre social rebel Modlizki. He is a servant who refuses to 'take part'; for example, when his master plays table tennis,

Modlizki does not 'play' but merely 'returns the ball'. He believes this attitude of complying with everything, 'but in a way that confuses those who give the orders', will lead, if carried out on a large scale, to madness and despair among the 'ladies and gentlemen'. Modlizki manipulates both Blau and some of his pupils to this end. He is also one of the main figures in Ungar's comedy, *Die Gartenlaube*.

The Class also has its comic elements, but it is a grotesque comedy that arises from figures who are so one-sided, so dominated by one element of their make-up (Blau by his belief in fate, Modlizki his 'rebellion' against the social order, Uncle Bobek his appetites) that they become almost automata. The comic aspect only serves to emphasise the bleakness of the world of a figure whose exaggerated sense of guilt almost leads to the destruction of his whole life, including the wife and child he loves.

Chapter One

He knew the boys were watching his every move; the slightest chink in his armour could expose him to disaster. In that year he was faced with eighteen boys. They sat in front of him at their desks, two by two, and looked at him. He knew disaster would come. He had to resign himself to appearing to be cruel. He knew that he was not. He was fighting for his livelihood, he fought for every day of reprieve. His severity was one element in a system designed to put off the end. He, the teacher Joseph Blau, had to gain time. Any day he gained might enable him, by summoning up all his strength, to obtain a mitigation of what he had brought down on himself.

He fought with all the means at his disposal to maintain discipline. Once it was relaxed, everything was lost. Once the first stone was loosened, the whole building would collapse. He knew he would be buried beneath the debris. There were examples he had heard of from which he had learnt that leniency and indulgence were not the way to keep boys in check. That had led to the downfall of other teachers. Goodness and compassion, so people said, were characteristics of the human race; if that was so, then fourteen-year-old boys did not belong to the human race. They were cruel at heart. He knew that once the restraint of discipline had gone, every-thing would be in vain, whether the reminder of the threat to the teacher's position or a plea for mercy. There would be no respite once they sensed, even for a moment, that their mock-ing laughter would pursue him when he was forced to flee, humiliated, head bowed, deprived of his livelihood.

The school was in a district of the town where the well-to-do part of the population lived. He himself came from a poor family. The boys were well-fed and well-dressed. He was aware of the freedom of movement and self-confidence a well-to-do background gave a person, if they enjoyed it from birth, and that it could not be replaced by education, not even by the acquisition of culture and wisdom. He was afraid this was where the first chinks in his armour might appear. He could feel the boys' eyes scrutinising his movements and his clothes.

He stood facing the class, unmoving, his back against the wall. His eye held them, individually and as a whole. He knew that he must not miss the least flicker of a smile, however secretive, on one of the faces turned towards him. It could be a smile of arrogance and the beginning of the revolt. If he saw it in time, he could extinguish it with a look. He could also find some excuse to punish it. The most important thing was to keep concentrating for every moment of the lesson on the goal of not letting discipline slacken under any circumstances. That was why Blau avoided the habit other teachers had of walking up and down the classroom. It broke the tension, transformed motionlessness into motion, it was a release and released forces he could not control. It blurred the boundary between authority and the uniform block of those subject to it, the system was not rigid any more, movement made it flexible. The two weights could not shift spatially without endangering the balance. He knew that at his very first step the whole class would let out its breath, their taut bodies would relax. In addition to that, his own fixed position offered less chance of exposing his movements to the boys' scrutiny than would be the case if he were walking up and down. Despite the danger of another pupil whispering the answer, he made the boys answer from their desks instead of making them come up to the blackboard, as was usual. That change, as with movement on his own part, would have created a new, disruptive grouping. The bipartite order would have become tripartite and the straight line of sight from them to him and from him to them would have been diverted by the third point, the third weight.

The classroom door was level with the first row of desks, facing the wall with the windows. The windows looked out onto the playground. Three paces from the desks, in front of the wall to which the blackboard was fixed, was the dais with

Josef Blau's desk. His desk was positioned at the edge of the dais closest to the windows. If Josef Blau, like other teachers, had gone across the room, through the narrow passageway between the podium and the boys' desks, to hang his hat on the coat-stand intended for the teacher in the corner between his desk and the wall, he would have had his back to the eyes of some of the boys all the time. He avoided this by going straight from the door up onto the dais and across it to his seat. In doing so, he described a semi-circle, not only in his forward movement, but at the same time on his own axis, so that he did not have to let the boys out of his sight. He signed the class register, then positioned himself by the first window in such a way that the wall shielded his back from being seen from outside. He stayed there, facing the boys, until the end of the lesson. He left the room in the same manner in which he had entered it.

His clothes as well as his movements could give the boys just as much cause for mockery, if not more so. Nothing, Josef Blau felt, was more suspicious to well-to-do people than poverty. Even their compassion had an element of arrogance. He knew that good clothes were essential for him, even if it meant he had to make sacrifices to acquire them. At the beginning of each school year he had a new suit made. But despite the most painstaking care lavished on every article of clothing, he was aware – and ashamed – of how poorly dressed he was the moment he entered the classroom. He was so disturbed by the fear that the material on the seat of his trousers or his elbows might be shiny that he pulled his sleeves in towards his body a little and kept his arms pressed against his sides during the whole of the lesson.

Almost without exception the boys were dressed in blue sailor suits with wide open necks plunging to a point above their stomachs. The open neck revealed part of the chest and the white, hairless skin of their bodies. They wore tight-fitting trousers, which sometimes stopped well above the knee, and short socks, exposing even more flesh.

The way the boys were dressed filled Blau with revulsion. He felt it as a rejection of him, of his whole existence, it seemed to be directed against him, to be intended as a challenge to him. He was small and skinny. Since he found anything which flapped loose disturbing, and also from a sense of order, he wore his coat tightly buttoned up. His had thin legs, and he even concealed the skin of his neck with a high, starched collar. When awake he was visited by visions, as embarrassing as they were tormenting, of himself in a sailor suit being discovered by the boys, who mocked and shamed him, not least because of his hairy chest, till he wanted to crawl away and die.

In the boys' eyes he saw the lustful desire to cross the barrier and come close to him. Since, as long as he did not lose hold of the reins, that was impossible by force, they tried it with cunning. They followed him in the street. In the long run it was impossible, whatever precautions he took, to prevent them from seeing Selma. They must know of her existence, and whilst they were looking at him, their teacher, with the taut expression of obedient attention, their minds might be indulging in lascivious thoughts about his marriage. They might be stripping him of the cover of his clothes, down to his gaunt flesh, and imagining him with Selma in those situations which brought him down to the level of a dog in the street. Once they knew Selma, once one of them had seen her in her close-fitting clothes which revealed her full, rounded shape, then these imaginings would have real flesh to feed on. They must not be allowed to see Selma. Like the commander of a besieged fortress, he must make the land all around, even fertile land, into a desert, using any means to render the enemy's approach as difficult as possible.

There must be no other relationship between him and the boys than the professional one. The professional relationship had its norms, its fixed procedures. Once he had abandoned the ground on which these norms operated, a return was impossible. The impersonal relationship, independent of the individuals behind the roles of teacher and pupil, would have been replaced by a personal, individual one, and that for good. He had to be ruthless when the boys occasionally tried to entangle him, like a fish in the meshes of a net, in a private conversation. When they approached him, as he stood leaning against the wall in a corner of the long corridor during the break between lessons, he would turn them away with harsh words. He was not unaware of the articles people he had known as a student had published on the relationship between pupils and teachers. But there was no choice. The boys possessed the arrogance of the well-fed, the self-assurance of the well-dressed, their laughter would have destroyed him if they had been able to grasp the weakness they suspected within him.

There was one among them who did not wear a sailor suit. His name was Bohrer, Johann Bohrer. His father was a clerk in a lawyer's office. Bohrer wore a brown jacket and long trousers. His sleeves had shiny patches at the elbows. His hands were not white like the other boys', they were red, as if swollen by frost. Josef Blau avoided looking at this boy or addressing a question to him. He felt that Bohrer might suddenly get up from his seat, go up to Josef Blau, his teacher, and pat him familiarly on the shoulder, to roars of laughter from the rest of the class. He was afraid of the possibility that the boys might compare him, their teacher, with Bohrer, with whom they shared the food they brought for the break because they felt sorry for him. No one could understand his fear as well as Bohrer. Although he suspected what the answer would be, there was something stronger than him, something that brought him to the edge of the abyss, that made him ask Bohrer what he wanted to be when he left school. Bohrer did not raise his eyes as he replied in a low voice, as if he understood the shame it would bring Blau, that he wanted to be a teacher. For a moment Blau lost his composure. He felt for the wall behind him. He closed his eyes. But already a rustle of movement had arisen in the class and reached his ear. Was this the end? Did the boys now realise there was hardly any profession open to a clerk's son who attended a high school than that of teacher? That Josef Blau's profession was a profession for poor people? Would they see them together from now on, Josef Blau and Johann Bohrer with his hands swollen by frost? Would the shame remain with him for good?

17

He pulled himself together, his eye turned the restlessness back into rigidity. He realised he would have to resort to harsher measures in order to give his authority a firmer foundation. He thought of the means available to teachers of earlier generations, when they still had corporal punishment. They could have the punishment on one boy carried out by another, thus at the same time creating disunity among the boys, playing one off against the other, just as fate, to whom all humans are subject, plays one person off against another. Corporal punishment was more than other kinds of disciplinary action such as official reprimands, bad marks, detention or lines. They were punishments that did not hurt, that the boys' arrogance could dismiss with a smile. Corporal punishment would have made the pupils' physical subjection to the power of the teacher visibly apparent. Blau respected the principles that had led to the abolition of such punishments. He would nonetheless have employed them, had they been permitted, because the boys too would surely have used such means to destroy him. He would not have hesitated, since it was a matter of his livelihood. He had to suppress fits of leniency if he did not want to give up the fight for lost from the very outset. Josef Blau knew that the final catastrophe was inevitable but he fought for every hour of reprieve. He did not know where the horror would start. Danger loomed on many sides, in the world of the school and in the other world, which was not part of the school. Contact between these two worlds would have increased the danger, accelerated the catastrophe. He was aware he was grasping at straws in fighting against his fate. But straws were all there was to use against the law that was against him in all its cruel harshness.

He left the classroom with eighteen exercise books covered in blue paper under his arm. He heard the babble of voices that arose the moment the door closed behind him. Josef Blau could not see the boys any more, but he knew they had got up from their seats and were crowding round the desk where Karpel sat. At fifteen, Karpel was the oldest. Blau sensed that the enmity of the pupils towards him united and multiplied in Karpel. If the end were to come, and if it started here and not at home, the initial impulse would come from Karpel. Karpel's face had lost the smooth, womanly look the other boys' faces still had. It was pale and narrow, the nose was prominent and there were blue shadows under his eyes. The woolly black hairs sprouting from his cheeks made them seem grubby. The idea that this pupil's body also already had male hair was disturbing, especially since Karpel wore the same low-cut suit as his classmates, as disturbing as the sight of a man dressed as a woman would be for a prudish person, since they would be afraid a part of the body with male hair might be exposed without warning.

Josef Blau felt the arrogance of this boy, who despised him, even if he had not yet expressed his contempt out loud. He was surely gathering his strength and his hatred of his teacher in order to let it break out when the time had come for him to give the others the sign to fall on their prey. The pupil had nothing to lose. If he was expelled from the school his rich father would find something else for him. But the teacher was armed. It was not going to be made easy for them under his gaze, which he never took off them, under his eye, which held and saw through them. Karpel lowered his head when Blau's gaze met his. He hid his fingers under his desk when the teacher's eye rested on him. Why did he not leave his hands, with their carefully manicured nails, lying there? What could the reason be for hiding them from the teacher's view if not because he knew that Blau's nails were not manicured, that the sight of his hands shamed the teacher and that the time to shame Blau had not yet come?

Josef Blau quickened his step. Already he could hear the noise of the boys approaching on the stairs above him. He went out into the street and stepped into the first entrance he came to. He wanted to let the boys pass him. Now they were coming out of the building. They did not see him, standing there in the dark archway. But he could see them, jumping down the steps from the school gate into the street, flexing and stretching their bodies. They swung their books fastened with a strap. They were standing opposite him, Karpel in the middle. Karpel said something and Blau, in the entrance on the other side of the street, heard the voices joined in laughter. Karpel stood there, his hands casually in his pockets, his books stuck carelessly under his left arm. That boy was experienced already. He had experienced forbidden lusts. Perhaps a woman even. Blau was ashamed of his pupil's experience. Karpel was not ashamed. Karpel took a piece of paper out of his pocket. It went from hand to hand. The boys laughed. Without doubt it was an obscene drawing Karpel was showing them. Perhaps even one portraying him, Blau, their teacher drawn by the experienced Karpel, in a situation which exposed him to ridicule. Josef Blau could not step out, right in the middle of the boys, and confiscate the picture. He would have been crowded in from all sides. Scorn and arrogance in all of them. He would have been greeted with laughter, since for a moment they would still see him, the subject of the drawing, as Karpel had portrayed him. Out here there was no order to which the boys were subject, no order which kept the place facing the boys ready for him. Out here, among people, buildings, cars, in the noise of the street, he would have been forced to create that order. They were standing, their order was dissolved, they were in motion. Out here their victory over him was easy. He did not intend to let them achieve it like that.

Josef Blau waited. When the boys had gone he stepped out of the dark archway into the street.

Chapter Two

He had to cross the town to reach the house where he lived. He and Selma shared an apartment with her mother on the top floor of a tenement block. The building was black with the soot from the railway station opposite. Only where the plaster had come off the walls were there lighter patches among the darkness.

The whole of that side of the street was lined with similar buildings. Every floor was inhabited by several families. Red bedding hung out of the windows. Fat women without hats, their hair sparse and dishevelled, their blouses flapping loose round their waists, stood in the doorways carrying jugs and bags. Josef Blau went into the dark entrance. A smell of dampness and food permeated the whole building. The sound of voices, drowned by the long-drawn-out whining of small children and dogs, came from every apartment he passed.

Selma and her mother were not at home. Josef Blau ate his lunch in the living room. Martha, the maid, seventeen years old, small and flat-chested, the daughter of a neighbour, served his meal. On one side of the living room was the kitchen. Beyond the bedroom was Selma's mother's room, a narrow, one-windowed room with its own exit onto the landing. The living room had two windows. At one of the windows was Selma's sewing table, where she had been working before she went out. There were pictures on the wall, one colour print showing a large assembly of men – a meeting of the Reichstag or a church council – and a few family photographs, a portrait of Selma's mother when she was young and a picture of her late father, a powerfully built man with a shaggy moustache. The curtains were white, the walls decorated with a colourful pattern painted on the whitewash. Despite that, the room did not seem bright. The soot from the railway station came in through the windows, covering everything with a fine layer which took the shine off the colours and made them dull, grey, the one merging into the other. It was as if the colours lacked life, as if they had died under the layer of soot. They did not even come back to life when it was wiped off the furniture, pictures and walls with a duster. The windows faced north. The light was refracted in the station, its buildings, tracks, sheds and coal bunkers, before it could reach their apartment.

After Josef Blau had eaten, he spread the boys' exercise books out on the table. He fetched red ink and a pen from a wooden shelf between the two windows. He cleaned the nib carefully on a piece of cloth he kept for that purpose and opened Blum's exercise book, the first in alphabetical order.

It was quiet in the apartment. Josef Blau could hear nothing apart from the occasional clatter, as Martha put one plate on another in the kitchen, and the constant jumble of noise in the house. He tried not to think of Selma, of Selma coming up to him and pointing at her body, which was growing daily heavier, to drag a word out of him which he did not want to say. She did not understand that it was good to say nothing, apart from what was needful, since one never knew whether words might not turn into curses. He wanted to make use of the time before Selma came back with her mother. He wanted to go through the boys' exercises calmly, book by book, mistake by mistake, to shut out everything else, only think of what was needful, required by duty, of the Latin sentences and nothing else.

He sat bent over the exercise books and drew red lines under what the boys had written. There were six simple sentences. But those who did not pay attention got caught in the traps the teacher had laid, one trap in each sentence. To his astonishment, Josef Blau saw that almost without exception the boys had avoided his traps. His astonishment was even greater when he noticed that all of them had fallen into one particular trap in the third sentence in the same way. He arranged the exercise books in the order in which the boys were seated in class. He was horrified. There was no doubt about it, they were all the same. Had the boys, under his gaze, which never left them for a moment, found a way of conspiring against him, had they used it? He realised that they were silently mocking him. He had proved weaker than their cunning. They sat there, only outwardly bent before him, only outwardly subject to him. The object of their cunning ruse was not to satisfy him with a correct piece of work, even if it was obtained by cheating. The object was to test him, his strength, his eye. He had failed the test. It could only make them bolder. It was doubtful whether Josef Blau could save himself, could suppress the imminent mutiny, even if he did manage to tear this plot apart the next morning and tried, with new, carefully thought out measures, to force the boys into subjection once more.

It was an underground conspiracy, a conspiracy under the desks, a conspiracy of naked calves when the upper bodies were bowed in obedience. There was only one possible way it had been done: the boys had put their legs together, stretched them forwards, sideways. The cribs were passed on and received stuck in their short socks and down the side of their boots. The rigidity and motionlessness was only above the desks, below the surface was movement and anarchy. His eye had no power underneath the desks. While the heads and chests obeyed, the naked legs were in revolt. It was the beginning. Discipline was crumbling from below, even while he was there, believing it was firm, believing no sign of movement could escape his notice. They did not fear him when he was standing facing them. What happened when they were removed from his gaze?

Josef Blau stood up. He went to the window. The tangle of rails as they converged in the station was spread out before him. He had not seen any of the pupils on his way home. They were not following his footsteps. But perhaps they were lurking round the house. Perhaps they were lying in wait for Selma, had already descended on Selma, whispered to her that he had a ridiculous nickname, that he was afraid of the pupils, but that the pupils would destroy him, without mercy, when the time came. Perhaps they had pushed pictures into her hand, pictures in which he, Josef Blau, was caricatured, was shown as a miserable, hairy bag of bones, perhaps together with her, who had been made gross and swollen by him. They would definitely sense that he was attached to her, that his life depended on her. The boys were cruel and lecherous. They would not spare Selma. Spurred on by the sight of her pregnant body, the boys' lecherousness would wallow in images of her intercourse with him, the consequences of which were visible. Perhaps Karpel, who was experienced in lust, was whispering to Selma that other men were stronger in their virility and that she, Selma, was beautiful, had a magnificent body and would only wither beside him.

He was the son of a court usher in a small town. He was skinny, yellow and pathetic. His skin was rough, as if it were covered in semolina. His bobbling Adam's apple stuck out of his scrawny neck like a second chin. He had never uncovered his body before her in the light. Her skin was white and smooth. Her body was rounded, with firm flesh. What did he want from her? He came up to her forehead, just below her fair hair, which was combed back and tied in a thick bun over her neck. When she walked, her broad hips swayed, like those of women carrying jars on their heads. Her red lips were always slightly parted, revealing the gleam of her moist white teeth. He knew that men turned to look at her when she passed them in the street. They were men with smiles on their faces, men who could make their flesh go rock hard when they flexed their muscles They were men who waved and smiled at women. Perhaps Selma was already comparing him with one who was taller, stronger, more virile than he was. Had she already realised how pathetic his body was and that his spirit was too weak to let him rise up and make her forget the feebleness of his body? He knew that he had to put up a fight if he did not want to lose Selma. Even if the man who would tear her away from him was bound to come, Josef Blau was determined to apply all his powers of reason and method to delaying the moment. He had to keep his eye on her, nothing must escape him, no change of expression, no look, he had to get to the deepest unconscious meaning of every word she spoke, every sigh she gave, if he was to see the sign that she was slipping away from him in time.

24

He decided to go and see Modlizki, to get him to find out the boys' plans and reveal them to him. The danger from the boys was the most immediate. The boys were driven by their hatred of him. Their hatred would make them overcome all obstacles. If they hadn't yet approached Selma, then he must prevent it, as far as possible. He decided to restrict the times Selma went out to the essential. No one was to see her, not the boys, nor any man. If the boys realised the victory they had won today, they would lose their last inhibitions. The awareness of their superiority would make them even bolder. They might attempt to enter the apartment when Josef Blau was absent. Selma's mother was no protection, she was hard of hearing. She only heard things that were bellowed in her ear. The boys might know that. They might have observed Selma out walking with her mother and heard how she had to raise her voice to make herself understood.

Everything depended on preventing the boys from realising the victory they had won. Everything depended on Josef Blau being able, by the way in which he showed that he had uncovered their plot in the morning, by the way in which he punished it, to transform their victory into a defeat. As long as he could still impose his will on them, as long as the boys, glorying in their victory and goading each other on, did not turn the covert revolt into open rebellion, as long as, when he entered the classroom, Karpel, Laub and the other boys did not greet him with open laughter.

If he could still hold them down with his eye, if they had still not openly rebelled, then his course of action lay clear before him. The uncovering of the plot must be done without fluster, almost without a word. There must be no hint of how close to victory they had been. He would stand in his usual place and the boys, at their desks facing him, would have to do six new sentences. Instead of a punishment for the plot he had uncovered, and to prevent any new, underground conspiracy, he was going to decree that the boys had to keep their left arms stretched out on the desk in front of them while they were writing, with their fingers curled over the edge facing him. Their right hands would be writing, their left hands stuck well

25

out in front of them, acting like a fixed anchor, inhibiting the movement of the whole body, even the underground movement, or at least restricting the mobility of their legs to a minimum. This decree seemed better than a punishment. A punishment was bound to make those punished all the more aware of the importance of the occurrence. It would not deter the boys, perhaps even tempt them to further provocation. Returning the blow would make the boys into one party in a conflict, himself into the other. The relationship between them should not allow such a parallel to be drawn. If he appeared to let the occurrence go unpunished, he would have uncovered it but have kept his distance, not been drawn into it; however, his new directive would make the boys' subjection to his will physically evident in a more meaningful way than could be achieved by any of the authorised punishments.

With care Josef Blau prepared six new sentences for the pupils to translate the next day. Again he took great pains, while keeping the sentences as simple as possible, to include in each one an unobtrusive grammatical pitfall calculated to demonstrate how alert the pupil was and how far it was his own work.

While he was weighing up different formulations, he heard Selma and her mother on the stairs. Selma's voice, as she tried to make herself understood to her mother, was loud. Usually it was a pleasantly deep voice, but now it was embarrassingly shrill. Her mother replied and, since she was incapable of judging the strength of her own voice, it seemed to Josef Blau to boom, deep as a man's voice, through every room of the building, as if amplified by the powerful instrument of the body from which it came, like the resonating body of a double bass. Josef Blau closed the exercise books. He felt he ought to run to meet the women, open the door, get them into the apartment as quickly as possible. He wanted to shut that loud voice off from the rest of the building, as far as the door and walls constituted an obstacle to it penetrating the neighbours' apartments. He stood facing the door and waited. Now the voices were there, the key turned in the lock and Selma and her mother came in.

Selma's mother collapsed onto the chair where Josef Blau had been sitting. Still sitting down, she unbuttoned her jacket and put her hat on the table in front of her. Her breath came whistling out of her nostrils. Along her upper lip was the dark shadow of a moustache. Josef Blau knew that any moment now she would address him and he would have to reply. Terrible though it was, he would have to raise his voice above its normal level, and still he would not be understood. Selma's mother would nod to him, as if she understood, just as she always did, because she refused to admit to her infirmity by having to ask a question. She would give him an angry look, as if he were speaking in a low voice, a lower voice than normal, just to annoy her, to show up her deafness. She did not realise he was using all his strength, she did not see how his cheeks went red when he heard his own over-loud voice echoing back to him from the walls.

Now she turned her glassy eyes on him, now she spoke. 'Has Bobek been?'

He shook his head, emphatically and strenuously, at the same time opening his mouth wide to form his lips in a mute 'No', underlining it with a gesture of dismissal. He wanted Selma's mother to understand his signs. He multiplied them, as if she could only understand this mute communication if it was exaggerated, like the human voice.

'Where can he be? He wanted to talk to you. You know why. Or have you forgotten?'

He had not forgotten. It was because of the money. He gave a series of rapid, insistent nods of the head.

She opened her mouth, as if she were gasping for breath and pressed her hands to her sides. 'My corset! My corset!' she said. 'I'm suffocating. No one'll come now. If he's not here by now, he won't come.'

She stood up and left the room. The door slammed shut behind her. Her voice could be heard in the kitchen and Martha's apprehensive reply.

Josef Blau stood at the window. He had turned away. He knew that Selma's mother wanted to make herself attractive to Uncle Bobek. Uncle Bobek was a cousin of her late

27

husband. She squeezed her body into the strait-jacket of her whalebone stays, forcing the weight of her breasts up to make her old woman's bosom appear desirable to a man. He did not want to hear about it, not even think about it. It seemed to him that what Selma's mother was doing was shameful and offensive, not only for her, but, in some inexplicable way, for Selma herself.

Selma came over to him. Her gait was heavy, as if her body were pulling her down. She was holding a little package wrapped in paper and smiling.

'Guess what I've brought,' she said.

He gave her a questioning look.

She opened the package. In it was a tiny knitted jacket in red wool with a matching pair of pants. She spread them out on the paper and held them up to him. He was about to stretch out his hand to touch the tiny things, stroke them, be nice to them, when he stopped himself. He clasped his hands behind his back. What was she doing? Did she not realise what she was doing?

'Oh God,' he said, 'you must not tempt fate, you must not!'

He looked at her as if she were causing him pain. Why had she done it? Had she not understood why he never talked about what lay ahead? Did he have to tell her in so many words, thus perhaps rendering everything he had taken upon himself vain? She was still holding her arms outstretched. Now she let them sink slowly. The smile left her face. 'We shouldn't talk about things,' he said haltingly. 'We shouldn't say anything so we don't spoil anything.'

He wanted to go up to her. He saw her eyes were filled with tears. Selma turned away and left the room. She went to join her mother in the kitchen.

Josef Blau watched her go. Was she not bound to think he was hard and unloving? He should have called her back, explained everything to her. But how was it possible to speak? A word, once spoken, could not be recalled. It set out on its way. It made the world different. It summoned up a fate that could not be halted. One could speak this word or that, one could take a step to the left, to the right, but once spoken, once taken, one could not withdraw the word or the step. Perhaps he could write it down, weighing every word before he put it on paper, reducing the danger, restricting it. He should write everything down for her, so that she would stop talking about the unborn child, stop bringing it into the world before fate had decided to embroil it in this world, before it was there. She was deciding its sex in advance, considering what name to give it. He erased every thought of it from his mind. He must not anticipate the happiness, which he felt as strongly as she did; he must not, by anticipating the happiness before the event, invite the retribution which he might thus bring down not upon himself or her, the guilty ones, but on the innocent unborn child.

What would happen was not determined in advance. He had created this child, he, the teacher Josef Blau, had had the presumption to be God and implant life. Everything could bring down retribution, on him, on Selma, on their new-born child, for fates were linked, one could drag the other down, our relationship to the power that sat in judgment was not individual, on the one side there was the power and on the other, like the totality of the boys in the class, was the totality of those subjected to it, whose fates were interlocked, intertwined. Perhaps it would emerge deformed from its mother's womb, branded with fiery birthmarks, with a bird's beak, a hare-lip, fish scales over its face, crippled, with a monkey's tail, a hunchback, two heads, four-footed like an animal, such as he had heard and read about. However hard he tried, he could not drive these images away because he knew that what was in his mind was there, in the world, and could become a curse. One had to cross out such thoughts, just as one did not tell bad dreams, so that evil would not be in the world, would not come to pass according to the old belief that sprang from an obscure sense of the interconnectedness of things.

If everything had been decided in advance, then one could have been free of care. If there were a fate, an unavoidable, predetermined fate to which one was subject, then one would have only been able to do and say what was already decided, and one would have done it without a care in the world. But there was no unavoidable, predetermined step or word awaiting one. It was not the case that one could take this step alone, say that word alone, and with every word, with every step fulfil the fate that followed from them. One chose the step and the word from among many. One overstepped a harsh, unknown law, to which one was subject, and stumbled into one's fate. One burdened oneself with guilt which one understood too late, or never. There was a cruel power which watched over the law and judged harshly. God, the guardian of the law, stood there like the teacher in school, but wreathed in oppressive mystery. He recorded the steps one had taken and pronounced the verdict. It was carried out on the guilty one and on those whom he had caught up in his fate.

If only Selma could understand, without him having to spell it out, that there could be no other plan, since every word, every step had a power within it which could be triggered off, without one knowing when or how, for good or ill; no other plan than to admit nothing except what was part of routine, regular, necessary. To eliminate, as far as possible, the unexpected, the unintended, both at school and at home. If one kept silent, only doing what was needful, what had to be done, one could limit the danger. If only one could hold one's breath, not confuse the course of events with one's own exhalations! The very act of breathing involved guilt. Like the desks in the classroom, the trees lining the streets, one should not act. But one breathed, spoke, acted, however much one's system limited it, and those who were linked to one spoke and acted, and it was possible that the actions and words would drag them all down into the maelstrom of fate. What was so terrible was not that one brought about one's own fate, but that at the same time one shared the blame for the fate of others, the fate of their unborn child, which Selma would not stop summoning up with word, thought and deed.

It had gone dark. Selma's mother came in with a lighted lamp. Josef Blau drew the two curtains over the window. There was no building opposite with windows from which people could have seen into their apartment, but still the windows with undrawn curtains made him uneasy when there was a light on in the room. He felt as if the room were no longer shut off, closed in, as if the light pouring out opened up the wall to the street, to an invisible crowd, like the fourth wall of a room on the stage. Selma's mother had taken her corset off. She was wearing a thin, bright-red dressing gown with wide sleeves which slipped back to her shoulders. When she raised her arms, her armpits were visible. Her arms were fleshy, the skin yellow. Round her waist the dressing gown was held together by a belt. Rolls of fat bulged over it. She spread the table-cloth. Selma brought in the supper. Martha had already left. She slept with her parents who lived in the same building.

Selma's eyes were red, she had been crying. She hardly ate any of the cheese on the table.

Selma's mother ate with noisy relish. After the cheese she took an apple. It crunched and squelched under her teeth. Head bowed, Josef Blau waited for the noise to die down. He wanted to ask Selma not to buy any more apples. He could not stand the noise. He felt the urge to get up and rush out of the room, he had to call up all his strength not to move a muscle, as if the slightest movement would set off an unstoppable series of further actions.

When Selma's mother had finished, he said, 'You've been crying, Selma.'

Selma did not reply. Tears welled up in her eyes. She hid her head in her hands and sobbed.

'She's afraid of the pains,' her mother shouted in such ringing tones Josef Blau was afraid people would have heard it in every apartment in the house. 'It'll be all right. She's strong and healthy.'

She clenched her left hand and rapped the wood of the table-top with her knuckles. She sensed the dangers her words invited and hoped she could ward them off that easily.

'If you knew how much she loves you. She doesn't want the boy to be blond, like her, he's to look like you! And you're not exactly handsome, are you? You don't even think so yourself.'

Selma nodded her head. Josef Blau understood her. She could feel his doubts about her; she wanted it to be ugly, to resemble him, with red-rimmed eyes, ears sticking out, a flat nose so that its father would recognise it. Selma's mother took a second apple. Josef Blau stood up. He left the table and went over towards the window. The dark lampshade cut a circle of brightness in the floor. The brightness did not reach Josef Blau. Selma's mother was sitting with her back to him. She could not see that he was speaking and would not interrupt the conversation.

'You're crying because you don't understand me, Selma,' he said softly. 'We mustn't say things. We don't know what we might bring down upon ourselves. We must wait, Selma, don't you understand?'

'I can't wait,' she said, raising her head. 'I have to talk about it. If I can't I'm afraid it will kill me.'

'Be quiet, Selma, quiet.'

'But who shall I talk to if not to you?' she said. She looked at him with her large eyes. 'I haven't got anyone else but you.'

His hand felt behind him for the window-ledge. There was someone else in her mind already. She already knew she did not have someone else. She was prepared to receive this someone else who would meet her, perhaps already had met her.

'What is this about someone else?'

'I have no one else but you.'

'You don't love me any more.'

'Who else would I love?'

'You didn't say you loved me. Now it's too late to say it.'

'Why won't you believe me?' she said and went over to him. Her mother turned round. Then she bent over the newspaper she had spread out on the table in front of her.

'Why won't you believe me? Oh, if only I could prove it to you. But I can't prove it to you.'

Josef Blau drew himself up. She was standing one step away from him. He could feel her breath on his forehead. His lips were twisted. He looked at her, unmoving, menacing, eyes wide open.

'But you can,' he said, 'you can.'

She bowed her head as if waiting for a judge's verdict.

Hesitatingly his hand, index finger outstretched, moved towards her head. Already his lips were forming the words he wanted to say. He did not say them, Selma's mother's voice trumpeted from the table, 'Old Skopak's dead!'

Josef Blau's raised hand sank down. Selma's mother stood up. Her chair toppled over with a crash. She bent down over the lamp to turn down the wick.

'How can I prove it?' Selma asked.

Blau was leaning with his back against the wall. He was not looking at Selma any more. His head had slumped onto his chest, his arms were hanging down. Now he scarcely reached up to her shoulders.

'Wear long dresses,' he said tonelessly, his left hand gesturing as if waving something aside, pushing it away. 'Down to the ground out in the street, that is sufficient.'

'People will laugh at me.'

'Good, good. Wear long dresses.'

Selma grasped his hand. Before he could stop her she had pressed it against her belly.

'Can you hear?' she asked.

'Seventy he was,' her mother shouted.

He freed his hand from Selma's.

'Go,' he said in an expressionless voice. 'If you love me, go.'

It was around midnight when he went to the bedroom. He had finished preparing the exercise for the next day and entered the carefully constructed sentences in a notebook with flexible black covers. His bed was beside Selma's. Selma was asleep. Josef Blau undressed quietly, so as not to wake her.

It was dark. The only light was the shimmering white cross of the window-frame. He stared at it. Josef Blau lay there, not moving. He heard Selma's deep, regular breathing. She had forgotten to say her prayers, although all he asked of her was that she should say the prayer she had said as a child. She knew nothing of the man she slept beside. She did not know that he lay there, night after night, fists clenched so tight his nails pierced his flesh, teeth clamped together. He was seeking a way to God to beg a postponement, a mitigation of what he had brought down on himself. God stood there like the teacher in school. He recorded the way one had chosen and His judgment was harsh. One thought one had brought blessing and in His eyes it was a curse, one imagined one was choosing life and in the eyes of the judge it was death. There was no physical way to Him. He who stood in judgment was invisible, but one had to find a way to Him to plead for mercy. It could only be done by force of thought, by straining every nerve, by superhuman concentration. One had to ransack the storehouse of one's brain to think up ways of calling on God, invocations thought up for the first time since the very beginning, invocations that could not be denied. One had to overcome one's body. It was good to suppress it by adopting painful positions, by tensing it convulsively, compelling it to remain excruciatingly immobile, to make the thought hard as a steel bullet.

In the darkness he felt for Selma.

'Have you said your prayers?' he asked.

She woke with a start. 'I did remember,' she said, 'but I fell asleep while I was saying them.'

'Say them now,' he commanded.

'Are you saying your prayers too?' she asked.

If he told her, would she not laugh and tell him he was like a fearful child? He was a man, he feared nothing, not God, not the boys, no one. If he wanted, could he not tie the sailor-suited legs to their chairs and perpetuate the discipline for ever?

'Your prayers are good,' he said. 'God would laugh at me.' And he laughed, a loud, cackling laugh, like a madman's.

'O God,' Selma said, 'the way you laugh! It's frightening to listen to.'

She thinks I'm mad, he thought. Why did I defy God? Now I've sent myself plunging into the abyss. Why was I ashamed to tell her everything?

Josef Blau had still not fallen asleep when the cross formed by the window-frame merged into the window in the dull light. He could see the building on the other side of the courtyard standing out sharply against the grey of the sky. He heard the first sounds as the building awoke. The walls were thin. Steps went up the stairs; a door was opened. It was the head waiter who lived on the second floor. Carts passed along the street on their way into the city. Someone coughed, gasping for breath as if they were about to suffocate. It was old Hämisch who was always sitting outside by the front door when Josef Blau came home from school. A tap was turned on. The water gurgled, it was as if the walls of the room were gurgling. Josef Blau felt the gurgling was never going to end. Perhaps another tap has taken over from the first, he thought. Taps are the first to wake. He was going to count, to see how long the gurgling would continue, but he stopped because he saw himself surrounded by the boys in their sailor suits. The boys were surrounding him on all sides. They were laughing. He was standing by his desk, but his classmates had all left their places. He hoped the teacher would come soon, then they would leave him and go to their places. He looked down and saw to his horror that he was not wearing a sailor suit like the other boys, but a humiliating waistcoat and long trousers and a heavy gilt chain his father had given him. He was the only boy in the class wearing a waistcoat. He wanted to run away and hide, but he couldn't. The judge had entered and now Josef Blau was in court. The room was like the room of the district court in his home town where his father had worked as usher. Behind the long table with the crucifix stood God. Oh, Josef Blau could see Him clearly. He had raised His index finger, as if He were threatening him. Josef Blau insisted to himself that he knew who this man with the raised index finger was, that this man with the chewed, wet cigar butt between his yellow teeth could not be God. He knew that it was Judge Wünsche of the district court and he did not need to be afraid of him any more since he was no longer the son of the usher, whom the judge could deprive of his livelihood, and what was a district judge, anyway, when there were judges at the provincial high court, the court of appeal, the supreme court, even the lord chief justice himself! It was his face, the district judge's gaunt, clean-shaven face with deep furrows in cheeks that looked as if they were made of wax, with light-coloured, almost invisible brows above colourless, unmoving eyes fixed on one spot, as if they could not move independently, but only when the whole head moved, with a long nose and ash-blond hair shorn close and brushed so it stood up. It was District Judge Wünsche yet it was not the district judge, he was much more powerful than Wünsche. Now Josef Blau was standing at the table. Beside him were the boys. He recognised the blond head of Laub next to him. They all put their hands on the table, Laub his white hands with the slim nails and the white half-moons one could see, Josef Blau his hands that looked like flat feet, red as if they had just come out of a Turkish bath, the fingers disfigured by chilblains and warts. Karpel and Selma were on the other side of the table. Karpel pointed to the hands lying motionless on the table, Selma looked at them, laughed and turned away from Josef Blau's hands and to the boys' hands. There was a rustle of noise in the room, like doves fluttering their wings, but it was the boys waving their hands. Nobody stayed with Josef Blau apart from Modlizki. Modlizki took Josef Blau's hands off the table and hid them in Josef Blau's pockets. They left the court-room and Modlizki laughed, as if some great joy had befallen him. They came to a wooden fence, it was the fence round the count's estate in Josef Blau's home town. On every plank were obscene drawings. Selma was standing there with Karpel, looking at the drawings. They went up to within a couple of yards of each one and then stepped back again, like someone enjoying looking at a painting. Josef Blau was going to rush over to them, but Modlizki held him back. He was still laughing. There seemed to be something he was pleased about. Josef Blau did not ask what it was, he did not want to know.

Chapter Three

The class had accepted Josef Blau's decree, which tied their bodies to their desks, without resistance. But now another danger was looming. In the next few days the school outing was to take place. The boys surely realised just as clearly as the teacher how special this day was, a day which, more than any other in the school year, fell outside the regular order of things. Being in an environment which was equally unfamiliar to both the teacher and the class, exposed to the sensual influence of nature, hot from the exertion of the walk, with the freedom of a constantly changing order, the excitement of the variety of visual impressions, and with the teacher isolated, alone among the boys between fields, woods and sky, which the class was bound to sense, all this made the dangers on that day more menacing, more diverse, more inexorable than on any other day.

It was impossible to calculate what might happen on that day. There was no timetable for that day, no order allocating a particular position, a particular place to the teacher, as there was in school. The class would sing, scatter, surround him, ask questions, go to inns for a drink; discipline would be relaxed from the very first step when they set off in the morning. School discipline was unsuitable for these occasions and Josef Blau knew of no other that was appropriate for such circumstances. Perhaps they had prepared mocking songs they would sing while walking or at the inn, songs mocking him and Selma, perhaps with the release of their energies the class would not be able to resist the temptation to lay hands on Josef Blau. They did not need to fall on him with blows, tear the clothes off him to destroy him, to make his position with them impossible for ever, all they had to do was to tug at him, pretend to be drunk and pluck his sleeve, take him by the arm and, ostensibly in the exuberance of high spirits, force him to run.

He had to recognise the danger if he was to counter it. If the boys had plans, he must try to uncover those plans. Then perhaps he would be able, by what he said and the way he acted, to prevent them from being carried out, to deter and confuse the boys by his knowledge. Modlizki knew Karpel. He had no choice but to go and see Modlizki, that very day. Perhaps Karpel took Modlizki into his confidence.

Josef Blau hurried home, the exercise books with the new test the class had done under his arm. As he was going up the final flight of the dark stairs, he heard voices coming from his apartment. He stopped and listened. He recognised the voice of Selma's mother. Uncle Bobek's voice answered. He heard the sounds, but he could not understand the words.

Selma was sitting at the table sewing. One corner was set for Blau's meal. Selma and her mother had already eaten. On the little red plush sofa, on the left as one entered the room, sat Uncle Bobek. His ample body took up two-thirds of the sofa. Uncle Bobek had his short legs stretched out in front of him and his head, which, in the absence of a neck, sat in the folds of fat on his shoulders, leant back, so that one was looking up his dilated nostrils with tufts of black hair growing out of them. His belly curved out like a globe. His collar was wide open, revealing the fat of his double chin. Selma's mother was sitting at the table, half turned away to face Uncle Bobek. Her left hand was on the table. She had her head on one side and was smiling. Her legs were crossed and exposed up to the knee.

'Here he is,' she shouted when Josef Blau entered. Uncle Bobek remained seated. He didn't like getting up, it took a great effort. He gesticulated with his tiny hand with its cushions of fat in Josef Blau's direction.

'Spring is coming,' said Josef Blau.

Selma's mother peered intently at his lips. Uncle Bobek twisted and turned his heavy frame, making the sofa creak. He smacked his hands on his trousers, stretched tight over his thighs. His hands were as small as a child's. Their disproportion to his body struck Josef Blau as grotesque. Moreover their skin was a delicate pink while Uncle Bobek's face, framed in a strip of black beard, seemed to glow blue-black from inside.

Uncle Bobek was about to say something. The words began deep down inside his body. They rasped inside his chest before they spewed out of his mouth. 'Excellent, Blau! Spring, summer, autumn and winter. The fifty-fifth time I've been through it now. Very interesting. Sometimes it's raining, sometimes it's snowing. Very important, very necessary. But why, I ask? Why, I ask you? Always the same. Necessary things, the seasons.'

'You're never satisfied,' Selma's mother screamed.

'Never satisfied? I think about things, that's all. Call it never being satisfied if you like. I don't mind. But I've been hearing what Blau's just said for so long now. "Spring is coming!" he exclaims. As if anyone would would find it surprising. Has the good Lord arranged it so as to give us a bit of variety? Holy Mother of God, that's the kind of variety you get in families where they have tripe every Monday, peas with ham on Tuesday and so on right through to the stuffed loin of veal on Sunday. Some variety!'

'Not in my house, Bobek. I don't know what made you say that.'

'I'm not talking about you, Mathilda dear. What I mean is, the miracle would be if God had only made one season, one where you didn't sweat, didn't freeze and didn't get rained on. It's necessary, is spring.'

Josef Blau had sat down. Martha brought his food. Blau looked at Selma. Selma lowered her eyes and shifted her chair closer to the table.

'Spring!' her mother cried, jiggling her free leg up and down. Then she closed her eyes in an expression of ecstasy.

Uncle Bobek made a gesture with his hand as if he were bowing.

'You see. The fair sex is against me and in favour of poetry. But I didn't come to talk to you about spring, Blau. I hear you're ready to sign?'

'Certainly, but . . .'

'It's a pure formality, you're not risking anything. I'll make sure everything's all right. A thousand crowns with interest for three months makes twelve hundred. Here,' he took a bill of exchange out of his breast pocket, 'I've brought it with me.'

Selma had put her sewing down on the table in front of her. There were round red blotches on her cheeks. Her mother was drumming on the table with the fingers of her left hand. Selma looked at Blau. Then she said softly, 'We'll need all that, especially at this time.'

'It will be there, Selma,' said Uncle Bobek, emphasising his assurance by placing his hand on his breast. 'I'll be in an awful situation if you don't sign, Blau, and you can't want that, surely? It's an old friend of mine who makes loans. He's willing to lend me the money. But two signatures, he says. Two signatures at the very least.'

'Twelve hundred in three months time?' Josef Blau said. 'And what if you're not in a position to repay the loan?'

'In three months time? Why shouldn't I be in a position to repay it, in three months time? But assuming I'm not, won't Berger listen to reason? After all, he's my friend. Would he be giving me the money if he weren't? I know what you're thinking, a bill of exchange's a bill of exchange and he'll forget our friendship when there's money involved. You're thinking he'll squeeze you dry with that bill of exchange. But it won't come to that, Blau. I know what I owe you, Blau, I won't leave you in the lurch, as God is my witness, or whatever else you'd like me to swear by.'

Josef Blau waved away his protestations. He took the form and signed it.

'It's a great danger,' he said, handing the paper back to Uncle Bobek. Uncle Bobek stowed the bill of exchange in his pocket.

'It's a lot of money,' said Selma. 'We'll never be able to pay it. Even if we sell everything.'

'You? It's me who'll be paying it, me. Who says you're to pay it? It'll be there, Selma, twelve hundred, on the day, and if the worst should come to the worst,' he raised his voice so Selma's mother could hear, 'if the worst should come to the worst, there's always our dear Mathilda.'

He gave Selma's mother a tender look.

'You have to keep a good hold on what you have when you're an old widow. You might need it, you never know when or what for.'

'Old widow, hahah,' Bobek cried, and his hands came slapping down on his thighs. 'Fresh as an apple, that's what you are. The men still run after you, Mathilda. D'you know what she bought today, Blau? It makes your mouth water.'

Groaning, he got up and went to the shelves between the two windows. His heavy tread set the glasses in the sideboard chinking. On the shelf was a small package, wrapped in paper. He unwrapped it carefully and took out a pink silk item of lingerie which he held up in the tips of his index fingers and thumbs so that it unfolded and hung down in front of him. It was a petticoat, low cut and trimmed with lace.

'Oh, don't,' said Selma's mother, her lips in a pout.

'How sweet,' said Uncle Bobek, 'how sweet!' and his eyes went from the petticoat to Selma's mother and back again.

Josef Blau stood up. 'Stop it,' he said.

He felt the sight was too much for him. Uncle Bobek ignored him. He swayed to and fro in front of the window, like a fat, bearded ballet dancer. He held the silk petticoat up against his body with the tips of his fingers. The flesh of his double chin pressed on the delicate lace of the low neckline.

'How sweet,' Uncle Bobek repeated, 'how sweet.'

He gave a lecherous smile. Selma's mother had put her head on one side, like a bashful maiden, and lowered her eyes. Her mouth was twisted in a smile that begged for mercy. Her daughter was bent over her needlework. Why didn't she leap up and tear her mother's petticoat out of her uncle's hands. How could she bear to see her mother made an exhibition of like that, her scheming designs exposed, ready for love in her lace petticoat and panties beneath the armour of her corset. Did she not wish the ground would open and swallow her up? Were they mother and daughter, or just two women, bound together by nothing other than the urgings of their sex? Could the one offer the pleasures of her flabby charms in front of the other, the fruit of her womb? Why did the other not cover her face? Was she not ashamed for her own body, which was about to give birth? Selma put a thread between her lips to moisten it, rolled it between her fingers, then held the needle up to the light and threaded it with a steady hand.

Josef Blau turned away and left the room without saying goodbye. He rushed down the stairs, past old Hämisch, who was sitting outside the house in the sun, the peak of his grey cap pulled well down over his eyes, and into the street. He hurried along as if, by fleeing the embarrassing scene, he could at the same time flee the memory of it. He wanted to increase the distance between himself and that room. Like Lot fleeing Sodom, he did not dare turn round and look back, as if fat Bobek were pursuing him dressed only in the lacy petticoat, and as if the sight would turn him, the teacher, into a pillar of salt.

Josef Blau made his way through the city. The main streets were full of people who pushed and shoved him. They crowded in front of the shop windows with the sun reflected in the large expanse of glass. He turned into a side-street. Here there was no glass glittering in the sun. The street was like a narrow, shady shaft let in between the walls of the tall buildings. No one bumped into him. There was no crush of people here, just the odd labourer, a woman carrying something, a clerk going home from the office.

He continued, heading nowhere in particular. He left the centre of the city and set out along the paths of a hilly park with many trees. Avoiding a clearing with the voices of children playing coming from it, he passed adolescent boys, with their arms round girls carrying briefcases, and nursemaids in colourful folk costume with wide starched white skirts. Josef Blau was tired from walking so fast and his head ached. He wanted to sit down on a bench, but all the benches were occupied by mothers and nursemaids with noisy children.

On one bench a white-haired man with gold-rimmed spectacles was sitting in the sun. His hat was beside him on the bench, his hands were resting on the handle of his stick planted on the ground in front of him. As Josef Blau approached, the man glanced up and Josef Blau found himself looking at a broad, calm face with short-sighted eyes regarding him dispassionately. Josef Blau decided he would sit down beside this old man. He would raise his hat and wish him good day. He would stay there until it grew dark.

Suddenly voices could be heard from beyond a curve in the path and a group of schoolboys with books under their arms appeared round the bushes blocking the view. Josef Blau could hear their loud chatter and unrestrained laughter. It might be boys from his class. They were too far away for him to see whether they were. If he sat down on the bench, they would walk past him. They might be smoking, ignoring the rule against it. It was not an encounter Josef Blau wanted, not on this day and not in the presence of this smiling old gentleman. His head was spinning from everything that was in it already: the bill of exchange, Uncle Bobek in Selma's mother's lacy petticoat and the threat of the school outing. Josef Blau had not forgotten the outing, but now the danger he had to prepare himself for once more loomed large and immediate. He had to go and see Modlizki. He could not put it off, it had to be today, now, while Modlizki was available, that Josef Blau looked him in the face and asked him about the boys' intentions.

He turned down a side-street which ended at a high fence. A narrow footpath ran along the wooden planks. Josef Blau kept his eyes averted from the fence. He knew that hearts and names had been cut into the wood, obscene drawings and verses scrawled on it with charcoal or chalk. The footpath led to a broad street. Josef Blau came out into it a few yards from the house he was heading for. He saw the iron bars of the gate with the bell let into the stone, the trees hiding from view the house set well back in the park, and the white, naked goddess with one arm raised in a casually graceful gesture over her head, emerging from the green copse on the other side of the gate. Karpel lived a few houses further in towards the city. The street was empty, there were no sounds coming from the houses and gardens. Just now and then a dog barked, only to fall silent again immediately. It was four o'clock. The masters were sleeping and the servants crept silently up and down the stairs, along the corridors and over the carefully tended gravel of the garden paths.

If Josef Blau pressed the bell, the gate would buzz and spring open. He would walk round the copse past the graceful goddess and see the castle-like building with the green shutters and the arched entrance with the broad stone steps leading up to it. Modlizki would be standing under the arch, motionless, as comforting as ever, and he would bow to Josef Blau, with nothing to betray the fact that he was the only person in the city who knew Blau from the days when he wore the cast-off jackets with the too-long sleeves, the waistcoats and long trousers of charitable inhabitants of their home town. Was this respect mockery? Would not face, figure and voice suddenly dissolve in a startling outburst of laughter?

Josef Blau pressed the bell. The gate sprang open. Once he had rounded the copse, he saw Modlizki, a black figure, in a high-buttoned waistcoat, his carefully done-up, soft bow tie under his chin as always. Josef Blau ought to have taken flight. Uncle Bobek was right. 'He has the evil eye,' Uncle Bobek had said. 'If I had a child, I would keep it away from him.' But what did Uncle Bobek know about him? What did anyone know about him? What did the boys know, into whose confidence he had wormed his way in order to destroy Josef Blau? Modlizki hated the social order, generally accepted as fair and just though it was, he hated the boys, for whom he did favours, and the masters he served, but his especial hatred he reserved for Josef Blau, for his wife, his child and everything associated with him.

Modlizki's goal was destruction. That Modlizki was of limited intelligence, uneducated, obsessed by confused ideas was no reassurance, for there was a logic to everything Modlizki said, a confusing, frightening logic, it all sounded as if it somehow made sense, it took hold of one, one could not escape it, one kept on coming back to get to the bottom of Modlizki's hatred, to soothe it, to moderate it. Perhaps the fact that one could find no arguments against it lay in Modlizki and not in what he said, in his eyes and his unmoving face and his posture and his deep, even voice, which spoke of everything apart from what Josef Blau wanted to talk about, avoided any memory of it. But the day must come when

Josef Blau could start talking about it, could find out why Modlizki hated him most of all, perhaps because Josef Blau, the companion of his youth, poverty and lowliness, had risen to a respected position. But Modlizki knew that those he had been put in charge of did not respect him. Perhaps it was that other thing, the old insult, which Modlizki had not forgotten, perhaps he was thinking of it whenever he spoke to Josef Blau, Modlizki had hated him since that day, that was when it had begun! As children they had been given meals in the houses of well-off families, in a different house each day, sitting alone at a bare kitchen table. But once a week – it was on Thursdays, Josef Blau remembered it perfectly – they met in one of the houses, Herr Wismuth's, he was a wealthy merchant, where they ate in the kitchen, then stood up and left, after they had thanked the old maid, who was called Genoveva, an unusual name, true, though not so unusual in that area that one would remember it just for that reason. Josef Blau was given a scholarship and accepted at the high school, and on the following Thursday the daughter of the house came to fetch him from the kitchen, where he was sitting with Modlizki, to eat in the dining-room off a linen cloth, while they left Modlizki outside. His father had been a drunkard, his mother did the washing in various houses. Josef Blau said nothing and obeyed. When the girl came to fetch him it never occurred to him that he could do anything but obey. She hesitated at the door and turned to look at Modlizki. Josef Blau looked in the same direction. And saw Modlizki's eyes. They were so full of hatred that it took Josef Blau's breath away. But already Modlizki had bent his head in dutiful respect once more. The girl was still hesitating, but she probably did not dare do anything without an express order from her father. Perhaps she had also seen Modlizki's look. She turned and left. Josef Blau followed her. He closed the door behind him on the kitchen and on Modlizki. That was it, Modlizki had not forgotten that on that day Josef Blau had been called up to the table laid in the dining room and had forgotten and offended his fellow charity boy and playmate. Modlizki remembered it and avenged himself by not allowing Josef Blau to talk about it and explain. He avoided the subject. He allowed Josef Blau to keep on coming to see him. Perhaps Josef Blau went not only to try and find out what Modlizki was planning, perhaps he felt the urge to explain himself, to appease Modlizki, but Modlizki did not want to be appeased, he wanted to go on hating.

Modlizki came towards Josef Blau, unhurried as always, his head with its black hair parted in the middle tilted slightly to the left. His large black eyes rested in unwavering earnestness on Josef Blau, his bearing was respectful, deferential, he was not smiling, not a muscle moved in the yellow face with the long nose. But this lack of animation was not calm, it seemed imposed on both face and figure by force, the deference a piece of play-acting, everything as if prepared for a purpose, frightening.

They went into the dimly lit, wood-panelled hall. Josef Blau sat down in a carved chair with his back to the window. It was good that the room was dark. It was easier to talk in the dark. He looked round the room. He saw mounted animal heads and weapons on the walls. There was a book open on the table.

'You were reading?' Josef Blau asked.

'A ridiculous book, in my humble opinion,' Modlizki replied. 'It wants to bring in justice and equality.'

'Why ridiculous?' Josef Blau asked. 'Why don't you sit down, Modlizki?'

Modlizki bowed. He sat down at a respectful distance on the edge of a chair standing by itself. He sat upright, not leaning against the backrest.

'I'm the one visiting you,' said Josef Blau, 'why all this formality?'

'I am well aware of the honour being done to me.' Modlizki's voice was deep and even. There was no sharp undertone of mockery.

'Oh God!' said Josef Blau. He looked at Modlizki. Modlizki's expression was calm and earnest. Modlizki remained silent.

'Why ridiculous?' Josef Blau repeated his question.

'It will not make any difference, in my opinion,' he said.

'Things should be left as they are?'

'It is not the most important thing, in my opinion.'

'And that would be?'

'If you took everything away from my master and shared out his wealth, he would still be a master. A master from whom everything had been taken away.'

'I don't understand.'

'I lack the ability to put it into words.'

'Go on, tell me, Modlizki.'

'Well, taking away their wealth is not what really matters, in my opinion. Perhaps one should stop them keeping their fingernails clean, changing their underwear, playing the piano and kissing ladies' hands, for example. If I were to have a revolution, that would be it. Perhaps there's no point in expropriating their wealth and property as long as that remains, all that fuss and bother, what they call the proprieties, etiquette, good manners, old pictures and so on. Those things distinguish them. They're seen as higher beings.'

Josef Blau thought of the white goddess in the garden as he listened to Modlizki's deep, restrained voice. 'You're part of it,' he said. 'You're not excluded.'

'My father was up a ladder when he was caught burgling,' said Modlizki. 'He fell off and killed himself. Ever since I was a boy I've had chilblains on my feet. And I'm not going to forget it.'

'No one can forget it,' said Josef Blau quietly.

Modlizki was staring into space. After a short pause, he went on, 'I think I'm not being boastful when I say that I'm a good servant.' He seemed to be thinking hard. Josef remembered that Modlizki had had to leave the Colberts, who had taken him in, partly as a foster-child, partly as a servant, because he had done something that contravened the standards of a respectable household. No one had expected it of Modlizki.

As if he had shared Josef Blau's thoughts, Modlizki went on, 'I know how to serve without a sound, I know where each article of clothing is kept and the kind of occasion on which it is worn. I know which set of cutlery to lay and which glasses go with which drink. The wine is kept properly. I am present when the lady of the house plays the piano in the evening. I hear what she plays, but in a way I'm not listening. The ladies and gentlemen listen and go into raptures. I am a servant. No one has the right to insist I go into raptures with them.'

Modlizki stood up. 'I refuse. My presence at piano-playing, conversation, meals and journeys is purely professional. I refuse to be personally involved. There was no other way available to me of making that clear to Herr Colbert than by allowing my sphincter its freedom while the meal was in progress. If people insist I stop being a servant, I will be my father's son. Herr Colbert was correct, in my opinion, when he described my behaviour as having the smell of revolution about it.'

Modlizki was standing in front of Josef Blau, his eyes fixed on him

Is he not right? Josef Blau wondered. The boys sat before him, well-fed, their hands neat and clean, with the arrogant smile of the self-confidence of the well-to-do playing round their lips. You couldn't expropriate that.

'You know Karpel? From my class?' Josef Blau asked. He stared at the floor.

'The young gentleman lives in this street, a few houses along. I have the honour of being taken into his confidence.'

'He's in my class.'

'That fact is known to me. He mentioned your name. I was aware that it was not appropriate to my position to indicate that his class teacher occasionally did me the honour of visiting me.'

'What does he do?' Josef Blau asked. 'What are his intentions?'

'The young gentleman is mature for his age. He likes to visit the bawdy-houses in Kasernengasse. I have several times had the honour of taking him there.'

It was good that there was no light on. Josef Blau felt the heat of the blood rushing to his cheeks. What was this? Modlizki could speak about it in a calm voice, without embarrassment? That confirms everything, thought Josef Blau, that confirms everything.

'Of taking him there . . .' he repeated out loud.

'I'm not kept and paid for feelings. I fulfil wishes. Including unexpressed ones. I'm not there to stop people going off the straight and narrow.'

It seemed to Josef Blau that Modlizki had given that last sentence more emphasis, spoken it a touch more sharply than the rest. He hates the boy, he thought. 'Modlizki,' he cried, lifting his hand as if he was about to hold it out to the other, 'we both went . . .'

'I'll turn the light on,' said Modlizki.

Josef Blau waved away the suggestion.

He bent his head down on his chest.

'The school excursion's soon,' he said quietly. 'Are preparations under way?'

'Preparations?'

'Preparations directed against me. They hate me. There's no doubt about it.'

'Nothing that I am aware of,' said Modlizki.

'Not aware of anything for the outing? But for other things? You must know.'

'I will know,' said Modlizki.

A bell rang.

'The master has awoken from his sleep,' said Modlizki. 'The master plays ping-pong after his sleep, to freshen himself up.'

Josef Blau held out his hand to Modlizki. 'You play with him?'

'I do not play. The master employs me to return the ball.'

When Josef Blau reached the gate, it buzzed and sprang open. It was six o'clock in the evening. The street was dark. There was no lamp until he reached the junction with the main road.

Chapter Four

The night before the outing was spent in invocations and prayers for the decisive moment, which he might be faced with the next day, to be put off, for the judgment that had been passed on him to be annulled, if that were possible. Selma was asleep beside him, unsuspecting, her lips half open so that her mouth seemed to be smiling all the time. Twice in the course of that night Josef Blau bent over her. He saw the gleam of her white teeth and felt her deep breathing on his face. He closed his eyes and stayed like that for a long time as she continued breathing and the soft warmth of her breath wrapped itself round his neck and cheeks. Selma's breathing was uninterrupted, it went in and out of the opening of her mouth in a regular rhythm; she had no fears. While he was struggling with fate, struggling not to lose her, she was resting in preparation for the coming day, patiently waiting for her body to ripen, like the fruits of the field. Josef Blau did not wake her.

He left the bedroom early in the morning. She was still asleep. He trod quietly so that she would not hear him, would not wake up and speak, would not, by some incautious word, call down anew the danger he had perhaps exorcised during the night. The morning was cool, but bright, promising a sunny day. Shivering, Josef Blau sat in a compartment in the last carriage of the train. He was alone. The boys and their teacher were not travelling together for the train journey, as was usually the case. Josef Blau had decreed that the boys were each to buy their ticket at the window in the order of their arrival at the station and then get on the train one by one, thus meeting up at random in the compartments. That would avoid a common rush for the train, which Josef Blau had observed as the first occasion for high-spirited disorderly behaviour on such days. They got off the train at a small station. Josef Blau stayed at the end of the platform. When it was empty of other passengers, the boys formed up in twos and waited for their teacher.

It was eight o'clock. The boys were lined up, parallel to the long, yellow-painted station building. In accordance with a decree from the teacher setting out the guidelines for the outing, which each boy had written down, they were facing the exit. There they stood, to the outsider a jumble of tall and short, to the initiate, above all to the boys themselves, invisibly linked in the stipulated alphabetical order: Blum, Bohrer, Christian, Drapal, Fischer, Fleischer, Fuchs, Glaser, Goldmann, Haber, Japp, Karpel, Laub, Lebenhardt, Müller, Pazofski, Reis and Vacha, all in some mysterious way bound one to another.

Josef Blau went up to them and gave the order to move off. Not walking in step, the boys started down the slope from the station to the road. Their teacher followed the procession.

Their steps never came together in the rhythm of the march. They were hesitant, uncertain, long and short steps beside each other. Villagers encountering the crocodile watched it pass with a smile. The boys avoided looking them in the eye. Embarrassed, they turned towards their teacher, hoping for the sign that would liberate them, the sign that would command the order appropriate to the march, the tallest at the front, the smallest at the rear, releasing the entangled forces, uniting the diverging individuals in one body, in an arrow with a hard point and a feathered shaft. Josef Blau gave no sign. His calculation had not deceived him. Their initial consciousness of strength and physical superiority had crumbled to embarrassed humiliation. The sun was shining down on the country road. The boys marched along in silence. They had their coats over their arms. Josef Blau was shivering after his sleepless night. He pulled his sleeveless jacket in dark-green loden tightly round him. Individual boys – Karpel, Laub, Christian, the giant Pazofski – turned to looked at him. Now they were talking among themselves in muted voices.

Beyond the village a gentle breeze, cool from the dew on the leaves it had brushed past and damp from the morning mists it had dispersed, was blowing across the open valley. Karpel took his hat off. The wind ruffled his black hair. The other boys followed Karpel's example. And as they turned off the road towards the woods to start the climb up to the place of pilgrimage in the hills that was their destination, Josef Blau was startled by a cry, repeated several times at the same volume by many others. Josef Blau had not recognised the voice. It could have been Fleischer's voice, or Christian's. But already it was all the voices. They sounded triumphant: left and left and left. Their bodies straightened up. The chorus gave the rhythm and now all the steps came together as one step. Josef Blau halted. Should he forbid it? He gave them a marching song to sing. He realised that what was inevitable must come as a command from him, he must seize the initiative once more. The boys sang and the procession moved swiftly along the gently rising path towards the woods.

Among the conifers the sun could not penetrate the dense branches. They were going uphill over slippery rotting needles. They had to avoid ruts in the track where the water had collected. They were breathing more heavily, singing more quietly. Josef Blau ordered a different song. Stones polished smooth by the rain stuck up out of the earth of the track. Bare roots lay across their path. The procession split up, faltered. The singing died away. Josef Blau ordered them to start again. It cost them an effort, their voices were tired, no longer maintaining the emphatic rhythm. He called out, urging them to hurry. According to the plan he had distributed the previous day, they were to arrive at their destination at midday. No confusion must be allowed to arise through not sticking to the timetable. No doubts must be allowed to arise as to the necessity of reaching their destination. Nothing of what their teacher had dictated to them the previous day must be changed. The hasty climb was to tire the boys out. When they arrived at their destination for lunch at the village inn, they must collapse onto their chairs exhausted.

The orderly march disintegrated. Some lagged behind. At the front Karpel was now walking alongside Pazofski. Laub, breathing heavily, his blond hair dishevelled, his face red, stopped and waited for his teacher. Josef Blau looked at him. Laub took a few steps forward, then halted.

'Line!' Josef Blau shouted.

They all turned to look at him. He saw red faces covered in sweat with mouths open, breathing heavily. They stood still and did not move.

'Laub, resume your place in the line.'

Laub obeyed. The crocodile formed up again. Shining through the trees they could see the light of the clearing above them. They had reached the top.

It was eleven o'clock when they came out of the trees. Spread out in the sunshine before them was a level landscape, green with meadows, just a few low hills here and there. Among low red tiled roofs rose the onion dome of the pilgrimage church, only a short march away. After the moist coolness of the forest, the class stepped out into the midday warmth of early summer. Josef Blau took his hat off as well. He wiped the sweat from his brow. Then he looked round.

He stopped. The line of boys halted too. Their heads swivelled to the left. They nudged each other and looked uncertainly at their teacher. Josef Blau stood there, motionless, his arm still bent with his hat in his hand. He put it back on and closed his eyes. Could what he saw really be there? The boys' giggles left no doubt. There, scarcely a hundred yards away to the left, spaced out in rows and stripped to the waist, arms raised and moving forwards, sideways, back in time with each other, was the class of Herr Leopold, who had been assigned to the school only a few days previously. The teacher himself, tall and slim and naked to the loins, stood in front of them, bending his naked body with them, his white flesh and blond hair shining in the sun.

Herr Leopold's class noticed Josef Blau's crocodile. The bodies ceased their bending, the raised arms came down. Josef Blau heard the sound of laughter. His own boys' giggles died away, their heads dropped. They felt the laughter of the others was directed at the bizarre, embarrassing formation in which they were marching along. Before even Blau could give the order, they started to move, hurrying to remove themselves from the eyes of the naked class as quickly as possible. Herr Leopold had his back to them. Now he turned towards them.

His chest was thrown out, the skin red from the fresh air. He waved his arm and nodded his head in greeting. The blood rushed to Josef Blau's cheeks. This could only be a dream, all of this, the naked bodies, Herr Leopold, the teacher, naked with his class, and Josef Blau's own class in front of him, heads bowed, hurrying on, only suddenly to throw off their own jackets as well and encircle him here in the meadow.

'Keep going,' he said, 'keep going.'

They started to run, tall and short in a disorderly rush, stumbling over stones, not trying to avoid them.

'Hello there! Hello!' That was Herr Leopold's voice. Josef Blau was running behind his class. Rising above the laughter that pursued them, a single voice could be heard. Josef Blau drew his head down between his shoulders. 'Thersites!'

That was the mocking nickname they called out after him. The ugliest man in the camp outside Troy! And the other one, standing naked on the grass in the meadow, was he perhaps Achilles? Or Odysseus when he met Nausicaa, arrayed in the splendour of beauty by the goddess Athene. How much longer would he be exposed to the looks that followed him? They were like weights attached to his back. For how many more steps would he have the strength to keep himself from falling?

A small stream crossed their path. It was deep, with a plank laid across it from one bank to the other. The boys started to cross it, one by one. Now he had to stop. There was no way forward. Now they would see him, see him alone, wobbling on the wobbling, bending plank, putting one foot in front of the other, waving his hands to keep his balance. He was bound to lose it, in full view of all those eyes at his back, to slip and fall in. The others were still standing there, watching them. Their laughter rang out again. Josef Blau and his class, who would never forgive him for the mockery, for the scorn they had suffered because of their teacher, kept their heads down. They were pushing and shoving to get over the footbridge. One loud, laughing voice was carried on the laughter to Josef Blau, his nickname again, no, no, a new one, inexplicable, devastating. Was it aimed at him, Josef Blau? Was this the end? Josef Blau raised his arms. They had all heard it.

'Theresa!'

The laughter broke off. The only sounds were the footsteps of the boys and the monotonous trickle of the water. Once on the other side, they all turned round. They were watching him, eyes wide, not in their marching order any more, but in a semi-circle facing the plank over the stream. They were all waiting for him, those in front and those behind. He shut his eyes. Slowly, unstoppably, the ground beneath his feet began to move. His bones had melted away. He was sinking straight down, into the soles of his feet. He heard a cry. Who was it that had cried out? Then the sound of many feet running. Faces leaning over him. Perhaps he had fallen in the stream. Someone was fumbling at his buttons to undress him. Herr Leopold's chest was close. In the valley between the swelling hills stood a single house all by itself. No one could see it apart from Josef Blau, for the sun made it as bright as the air.

Josef Blau opened his eyes. Herr Leopold was bending over him. He had put a jacket on over his naked flesh. It was hanging open. The boys were standing round him in a wide semicircle, Blau's pupils and those of the other teacher, the latter as naked as their teacher. Josef Blau felt his coat. It was dry and still buttoned up. Just his high, stand-up collar had been undone and his tie loosened.

'There,' said Herr Leopold, 'it's all over now.'

Josef Blau stood up. He tried to do up his collar and tie. They were all looking at him. Every time he thought he had fastened his collar, the collar-stud slipped out of his fingers. He looked round. He was encircled on all sides. Herr Leopold followed his look. Josef Blau blushed.

'Leave your collar open, Herr Blau,' he said, 'and stay there until you fell better. You fainted from going too fast, that's all it was, Herr Blau. Nothing to worry about.'

He spoke calmly, in a pleasant voice, it was impossible to contradict him. But why didn't he button up his jacket? And why had the boys not got back into line? He had to put a stop to this. He stood up. Herr Leopold wanted to help him, but he was already on his feet. First of all the class must form its line again, then he would fasten his collar.

'Your pupils will see you get to the station, Herr Blau. Take it slowly. You should go home and lie down.'

'No, no,' said Josef Blau.

'You can't continue with the walk. Someone must go with you. One will be enough, the rest can join my class. Which of you will accompany Herr Blau to the station?'

'I will,' said Karpel, stepping forward.

Was he trying to make fun of him, or had he realised it was an opportunity to be alone with his teacher, in the forest, without witnesses? Did he intend to use obscene, insulting expressions, expressions from the bawdy-houses in Kasernengasse, to mock Selma for being his wife? No, no, not with that boy, not with any of them, by himself, let them stay with Herr Leopold, unclothe their bodies, perform pagan dances with him, naked in the meadow.

'Thank you, Herr Leopold, but I will go by myself. Make way there. All move over to the left. Thank you. I'm going now.'

He doffed his hat and left. He did not turn round until he was among the trees. He held himself upright and placed his feet on the ground with his toes pointing inwards. In the forest he sat down on the smooth stump of a tree that had been felled. Now they couldn't see him, but he could see them. They were lying in the grass round Herr Leopold, smoking.

Josef Blau looked along the track he was going to walk calmly down through the woods to the station. The dangers of school were behind him for one more day. Let them stay with Herr Leopold and do as he, or they, liked. Now it was he, and not Josef Blau, who would go to the inn with the schoolboys and make his way back in the evening through the darkening forest with boys inflamed by drink. Let him see how he dealt with that, Herr Achilles! He could hear the voices from the meadow and turned to look.

The boys were standing with the teacher, ready to set off. Now they were heading towards the footbridge, in no particular order, beside, behind each other as chance or choice dictated, the teacher in the middle, hatless, towering above even the tallest by a head. When they reached the track, one detached himself from the group and set off towards the woods. Josef Blau stood up. He recognised Karpel. What were his intentions? Had he, feigning concern for his teacher, obtained permission to hurry after him? Karpel was approaching quickly. He was running more than walking. Soon he would be there with Josef Blau, if he did not hurry off, flee from his pupil down the hill. But would Karpel not catch him up in a few minutes? He had to stay where he was, stand in Karpel's way, exploit Karpel's surprise, who would not be expecting him there, confuse the pupil by his posture, his look and, if there were no other way, drive him back by the power of words which would quickly show the pupil that the teacher knew his secret, that he was in the teacher's hands, perhaps with one single word that he could hurl at the pupil: Modlizki! He could already hear Karpel's hurrying steps. But would Karpel let himself be scared off if he was face to face with his teacher alone?

Karpel came into the forest. Hidden by the broad trunk of a tree, his teacher was only a few yards from him. Karpel slowed down. Took a few more hesitant steps. Then stood still. He was looking straight ahead, as if he were afraid to look round. Josef Blau did not move either. Now Karpel looked to the left, to the right, now he turned round. His teacher was standing behind him, on the right, only half concealed by the tree, rigid, his arms raised. His fists were clenched, his lips pressed tight together, his wide-open eyes fixed on his pupil, whose own eyes were cautiously feeling their way towards him. Could he not see his teacher? The blank look moved on past him, was lost in the trees. Karpel turned away and, as if he were fleeing from a terrifying vision, ran, head bowed, down the steep track, over smooth-washed stones and bare tree-roots, without looking round. And suddenly he began to sing, a song they had sung on the way up, the same song over and over again. The sound echoed back from the forest, amplified.

Josef Blau left his hiding place. He followed Karpel down the track. He could hear the boy's voice below him. He walked calmly, since he knew that Karpel was in front and he did not have to fear he might lie in wait for him in the bushes.

He could not see Karpel at the station. Only when he looked out of the train at the platform did he see him appear from behind the station building. Karpel did not look up. He walked slowly to the train and got into a second-class compartment.

Chapter Five

At first Josef Blau did not understand what was going on. Bobek was sitting there in his shirt-sleeves, leaning back, with no collar and his waistcoat undone. Selma's mother was standing beside him, her face red, her hair tousled. Her blouse had come out of her belt. Selma came towards him. His eye ran down her figure. She was wearing a long skirt, which covered her legs down to her shoes. Selma blushed. She bowed her head.

'He wants to celebrate,' she said. 'He sent Martha out to get some wine, the joint of veal he brought himself. Mother had to roast it for him. I've kept some for you.'

'Here he is!' Uncle Bobek cried. 'Back from the outing? Fresh air gives you an appetite. Sit down, Blau. You must join us in our little celebration. Without you we wouldn't have the money, would we, Mathilda? What's the point in keeping it, I say, what's the point? Sit yourself down, Blau, here, beside me, here, on the left where the heart is.'

He put a heavy arm round Josef Blau's shoulder and pushed him down onto a chair.

Selma set a plate of roast veal in front of him.

'Eat, my boy, eat and drink.' Bobek clinked glasses with him and insisted he drink. 'To . . . to . . . well, to everything, are you with me? To everything, Mathilda.'

Selma's mother emptied her glass in one gulp.

'There's a lot to celebrate,' said Bobek, 'a lot to celebrate. Just look at her, yes, her sitting there, isn't she as lovely as a young girl?'

'Bobek . . .' Selma's mother protested.

'As God's my witness, she is. Like a young girl. She's deaf, you say? If you want to whisper sweet nothings in her ear, you'll have to shout, that's what you're thinking. Come on Blau, admit it, that's what you were going to say, wasn't it?' He put his face close to Josef Blau's. The sour reek of wine wafted across him.

'Not that I am aware of,' Josef Blau said.

'She isn't deaf, I tell you! Healed, I tell you! Only an hour ago you could smile and say "old cow" and she assumed it was a term of endearment. But just as wine loosens some people's tongues, it loosens others' ears, hahaha, it's loosened her ears.' He slapped his thighs. 'Just listen, you, Blau, and Selma, we'll have a little test. Can you hear me Mathilda?'

'You go on as if you could fire a gun right next to me and I'd never hear it,' Selma's mother said.

'No harm meant, Mathilda dear.' Uncle Bobek patted her on the shoulder. 'Listen, Mathilda dear, I'm going to say a word. What, say it? I'm going to whisper it, hahaha, no more than breathe it, and you'll repeat it, loud and clear. All right?'

Selma's mother nodded.

'Off we go then,' said Uncle Bobek. 'But first I need a drink to wet my whistle. I mean to whisper like an angel.'

He clinked glasses with Blau and Selma's mother. Selma was sitting with her back to them, sewing.

'Here it comes, then,' said Uncle Bobek. He pursed his lips, his eyes were wide open with the effort. 'Chamber pot,' he whispered in tender tones.

'Chamber pot!' Selma's mother shouted.

'Hahaha! Passed with flying colours,' Uncle Bobek cried, throwing himself back as he laughed and making his chair creak in protest. 'Did I not say it with the voice of an angel? Did I not fill it with love, Mathilda?'

Proudly Selma's mother looked at them all, one after the other.

Josef Blau pushed his empty plate away. At first he hadn't wanted to eat, but the wine had given him an appetite, and now it was making him tired. He knew that if he closed his eyes he would fall asleep. It was good that he had not stood in Karpel's way. Josef Blau would have raised his arms, opened his mouth wide, given him a fearful look and cried out in an even more fearful voice, 'Modlizki!' But then Karpel would not have run away, Karpel would have followed his teacher as he strode out, always one step behind him, wringing his hands and begging for mercy. But Josef Blau would have remained hard, only turning round from time to time, stony faced, to reject his pleas. He would not have let his pupil wring an agreement out of him to spare him, even though Karpel would have followed him here, to the house where he lived, perhaps even into the apartment, where this scene would have transformed Josef Blau's victory into a humiliating defeat. Bobek might perhaps have asked the pupil to stay, to join in the party Bobek was giving for himself, for his own excessive fondness for food and drink, and Karpel would have witnessed this scene, witnessed his teacher's drunkenness as well. For the unaccustomed wine was going to his head and pouring into his limbs, which felt strangely weightless. He tried to ignore Bobek, when he urged him to drink, but it was difficult not to respond to the fat man's toasts. He could be very insistent and there was a danger he might lash out wildly, like an animal, if provoked. He saw Selma bent over her needlework. She did not look up. She was ashamed of him. The way he was behaving he could be putting everything at risk, he was not offering enough resistance to pleasure – no, he wasn't, however hard he tried – and forgetting what he should never forget, namely that every word he spoke, every step he took was irrevocable, placing him and those connected with him at the mercy of fate. He said softly, 'Judgment,' but today it had no power, it was a word, nothing more, it did not compel him and he could not compel it to be as terrifying as usual.

Uncle Bobek had put his right hand down the low-cut back of Selma's mother's dress. 'Just a slip of a girl, that's what she is, as God's my witness. Don't let me hear anyone calling her an old cow, hahaha, she's as frisky as a young heifer. Is there any of that roast left, Martha?' he called out to the maid. 'Over here with it, child.'

Martha brought a plateful of roast veal, which she placed on the table in front of Bobek. Bobek patted her on the back. Martha stood there, trembling, and didn't dare move until Uncle Bobek had set about the meat.

First of all he wiped his knife and fork clean on the tablecloth, then he cut the meat up into large chunks. He ate noisily, with his mouth open. From time to time he wiped the fat off his moustache with the fleshy back of his hand. His eyes were gleaming. He chewed at the bones with his teeth, then slurped the marrow out of them. He was panting and wheezing. From time to time he leant back and gurgled with pleasure. Then he took his glass and washed the half-chewed hunks of flesh down into his belly with the wine.

Selma's mother had got up and left the room. Now she came back, a bottle of kümmel in her hand.

'You've got some kümmel, Mathilda? What a girl! A man would be in good hands with you, eh?'

A dreamy look came over Uncle Bobek as he stared at the glass Selma's mother placed in front of him. Then he lifted it up and drank. He shook himself and put the empty glass back down on the table with a sharp tap.

'Brrr. That sorts your stomach out, that keeps you young. A glass or two of that after every meal and after every bottle. Him too.' He pointed at Josef Blau. 'Drink to my good health, Blau. There you are, it burns your throat clean, I say. A man who drinks a kümmel a day until he's eighty will live to be old, I say, haha! Where did you get it from, Mathilda? From your secret drawer?'

'Just in case,' Selma's mother shouted.

'We're going to have to inspect that secret drawer of yours, Mathilda, and see what you keep there just in case. Out with it, with everything, I say.' He rolled his eyes and leant over the table towards her. 'Why are you keeping it locked away? Here,' he shouted, 'here!' and he thumped the table with his fist. 'Out with it! Pay, pay!'

'Maybe,' said Selma's mother, giving him a smile. Uncle Bobek lowered his head. Then he poured himself and Josef Blau another glass.

'He's pouring it all down his throat, stuffing it into his belly, all the money I stood surety for,' Josef Blau thought to himself.

'Drink,' said Uncle Bobek.

'It won't come to the worst,' he thought. 'Bobek said Selma's mother will pay, if need be.' He nodded at Selma.

'Kümmel!' said Uncle Bobek. 'Caraway! It just grows and someone comes and boils it and makes schnapps out of it. Yes,

yes. Do you think I wouldn't have asked for some if dear Mathilda hadn't brought it herself. It's part of the meal. When we got married, Martha and I – my late wife, not Martha here –, we had the wedding feast at the inn in Puhonitz. Yes, yes. What a woman! A weepy one she was and always in the kitchen. We sat down to the meal, thirty of us, young lads, women, even the old folks kept their end up. Soup, veal, pork, chickens, two calves and two fat pigs, the whole lot from the head to the tail, dumplings to go with it and barrels of sauerkraut. And first beer, then schnapps. And no holding back, hahaha! I was at the head of the table with Martha. She ate nothing, my plate was never empty, and every bite was washed down with a bucket of beer or a tumbler of schnapps. Everyone was screaming and shouting, you couldn't hear yourself speak, what with the creaking of jaws, the clicking of tongues, the smacking of lips. The Puhonitz inn is well-known far and wide. Martha was nineteen to the day, right from the start she had red blotches on her cheeks, didn't dare look at me, not a word, just sat there staring at the table. When they made jokes about youknowwhat, the way they do with newly-weds, she blushed to the roots of her hair, didn't laugh, just sat there saying nothing. Sometimes I sensed she was looking at me out of the corner of her eye, but when I tried to give her a cuddle, she pushed my hand away. The others had already got up and were dancing, they were clearing the tables away, when there was shouting from outside, a cart had arrived, the lads from Holitz, twelve of them, come to celebrate my wedding. By then I couldn't stand, so the lads came over and sat round the table. Soup and veal and pork and beer was served up again, and I began at the beginning again. Martha just sat there, saying nothing. The Holitz lads raised their glasses, "Drink to them," I shouted, but she only nodded. Then the innkeeper comes up, whispers in my ear. "What!?" I said, "no kümmel, no schnapps?" Then the Holitz lads shouted that they wanted schnapps, the meat's fat, they wanted to drink the health of the happy couple, they shouted. "I'll never be able to show my face in Holitz again," I said to Martha, "if there's no schnapps. The shame of it!" So the landlord sends round to everyone in the village, while I drink to the Holitz lads with beer, one eye on the door all the time to see whether any kümmel's arrived. Someone in the village must have some kümmel, I think, but the landlord stands by the door and just shrugs his shoulders. Then the Holitz lads start to sing and when they've finished, I start another song, to pass the time. I turn round to Martha, she might have thought of it, I think, and I see the girl sitting there, in her wedding dress and myrtle wreath, crying. The tears are running down into her mouth. I feel sorry for her and I say, "Don't cry, Martha, the kümmel will come." And there's the landlord, he's got some from a farmer who kept a cask, just in case, like Mathilda here. But Martha, God rest her soul, went on crying. God forgive me, but she always was a weepy one, there was no reason to cry any more. But no one apart from me knew that she didn't touch a drop on her wedding day. The lads thought she was drunk, so that was all right.'

Bobek was lost in thought.

Selma got up and fetched a cloth. Uncle Bobek had knocked a glass of schnapps over on the table. To Josef Blau she seemed taller than usual in her long dark dress. Now no one will follow her in the street, he thought, everything will be all right. After our encounter today Karpel will not dare to go near her, no one will. That night, he decided, he would drag all her secrets out of her. That night he would talk to her. He loved her, but until now she had not known, he himself had not realised until now. He would stand up and put his arm round her, here, in front of them all, he could stand as steady as always. The wine had made him lighter, but he wasn't swaying. 'Selma,' he could say, 'the kümmel will come.' Joyfully, lovingly she would look at him as never before with her bright, glistening eyes, her lips parted to reveal her shining teeth. What would she reply? 'I thank you.' That would be it, perhaps.

Josef Blau heard a clatter, a crash of broken glass. Standing up, Uncle Bobek had overturned his chair. He tried to hold on to the table and his hand had knocked the bottle of schnapps over, which smashed an empty schnapps glass as it fell. Selma's mother supported him and he flung his arms round her neck. She led him to the sofa and, with a loud snort, he collapsed onto it.

'That's enough,' she cried. 'Take the glasses away, Selma.'

'It's six o'clock,' said Selma, looking at Uncle Bobek. He had closed his eyes.

'He'll sleep here,' her mother said.

She took his cigar, which had gone out, away from him and brushed the ash off his waistcoat. While she was doing that, Selma took the plates and glasses off the table and folded up the table-cloth. Martha, who had been asked to stay a little later than usual, brought a damp cloth and cleaned the sticky liquid off the table. Selma opened the window.

Josef Blau seemed to hear a loud roaring in his ears, a see-saw of noise that lifted him up then let him down. But now he thought he could hear steps. They were coming up the stairs. There was a knock at the door. Josef Blau opened his eyes. He stood up.

'Come in,' Selma called out.

The door opened. Josef Blau held on to the backrest of a chair. It was Herr Leopold, the teacher, who came in. He had changed, now he was wearing a dark-brown suit with a stand-up collar and a brightly coloured tie. The corner of a brightly coloured handkerchief was hanging out of the breast pocket of his jacket. Josef Blau saw Uncle Bobek's undone waistcoat. He wanted to hurry over and nudge Uncle Bobek, make him aware that his dress needed adjusting, but Uncle Bobek had already opened his eyes and was making heavy weather of doing up his buttons.

Now he heard Herr Leopold's calm voice, the voice it was impossible to resist. He wanted to know whether Josef Blau had had any problem getting home.

'What's this?' Selma asked. 'What happened?'

'Just a minor fainting fit,' said Josef Blau. 'It's all right now.' When he heard his own voice, it was like that of another person. It was cracked and rough and sounded high-pitched compared with Herr Leopold's rich, deep voice.

Now Uncle Bobek got up. He went over to the visitor, supporting himself on the backrest of a chair and the edge of the table. Herr Leopold did not shrink back at the reek of wine and schnapps Uncle Bobek breathed over him.

'Bobek,' said Uncle Bobek. He held out his hand and took Herr Leopold's in a firm grasp. Herr Leopold said his name.

Uncle Bobek introduced him to the women, still keeping the visitor's hand firmly in his own.

'We've been having a little party, as you can see. You must forgive me, but when you get to my age, you like to make yourself comfortable.' He pointed at the roll of bare flesh that was his neck, his shirt-sleeves and undone waistcoat. 'Do sit down, Herr Professor, here, here. And you, Mathilda my dear, how about . . . can you guess? A cup of coffee, I think that would be a good idea.'

Selma's mother left the room. 'Excuse me a moment, Herr Professor,' she said.

'Coffee, Herr Professor,' said Uncle Bobek, who had sat down in his chair again, 'coffee does you good at any time. You can drink it whenever you feel like it. We've just finished a little party – *en famille*, our dear Mathilda does these things excellently – and you've had a long walk. It'll do us all good.'

Herr Leopold was sitting next to Selma. He looked at Selma, who had moved her chair right up to the table. Josef Blau could not fail to notice that she was blushing. Was she ashamed of her long skirt, of her body that bore Josef Blau's child? Uncle Bobek talked uninterruptedly. Sometimes his tongue would lose its way and feel along the roof of his mouth before it found the word it needed. Herr Leopold looked as if he was listening. But was he not secretly looking at Selma? His face was sunburnt. He was healthy, had broad shoulders. His chest bulged and was free of hair. Josef Blau had seen it: Leopold, the teacher, naked, the sun on his back, standing in the grass with the boys round him, naked and moving their bodies like sun-worshippers. Now he was sitting next to Selma. Perhaps she could feel through his clothes the smell of air, woods and grass on his skin.

Herr Leopold smiled. Uncle Bobek was talking. He used

refined expressions. Everything he said made Josef Blau look ridiculous. He talked in a loud, wheezing voice.

'If one knows how to prepare it,' Josef Blau heard him say, 'that is the important thing. It must not be allowed to boil, no, on no account. You just bring it to the boil, you understand, just bring it to the boil so you're left with a rich decoction, not some watery black liquid. Just imagine you've eaten and drunk. Your brain's tired, and all hell's let loose in your bowels. You drink a little cup, your bowels are back in order, this to the left, that to the right, your brain clears. You can drink it on an empty stomach, it warms you up, promotes the circulation of the blood. Or do you not agree, Herr Professor?'

'It is certainly less harmful than beer, wine or schnapps.'

'There you are. You've hit the nail on the head, Herr Professor. That's what we should be aiming at. The eradication of alcoholism. Alcoholism is destroying the nation. Now an educated man drinks a glass of beer, or two or three, a bottle of wine and a kümmel now and then. And quite right, too, Herr Professor. But the common people are so ignorant. Where I come from we had a filthy pig, a war veteran, disabled, who drank methylated spirits by the tumblerful. An exception? An everyday case, I tell you. The eradication of alcoholism, that's what we should be aiming at if we want a healthy nation. Just look at the economy, trade and commerce, industry . . . we must fight against it.' He made a vain attempt to stand up and looked round the room, demanding agreement.

Herr Leopold laughed out loud. 'I think you should choose another topic, Herr Bobek. Something that will interest the lady of the house.' He gave Selma a smile. 'Alcoholism, that's something for men to talk about.'

'I was just expressing my humble opinion, just saying what I think,' said Uncle Bobek, hurt.

'He's been drinking,' said Selma, without looking up.

'Oh, I understand.' Herr Leopold laughed, showing his white teeth, and looked at Uncle Bobek with no sense of embarrassment. Selma's mother put coffee pots and cups on the table. The new teacher was sitting between her and Selma. Uncle Bobek sat down on the chair next to Selma, so that

Josef Blau was sitting between Bobek and Selma's mother. Uncle Bobek cut off large hunks of bread over his coffee pot and let them fall into the coffee. Josef Blau did not dare look up. He could have stood up and gone away, but the shame would have remained. Did Herr Leopold not have a strange gleam in his eyes? Why had he come? To see Josef Blau? Selma was silent. The new teacher might well be prodding her with his foot under the table, giving her secret signs. He was handsome, tall, a real man, a man for Selma, taller than she was, his arms rounded and hard. Perhaps when he got up to leave, she would follow him. How they slurped their coffee, Uncle Bobek and Selma's mother, the new teacher couldn't help but hear it. Should he knock the cups out of their hands? They were talking, a confused jabber of words. Josef Blau ought to join in, he ought to say something, he had been forgotten. They were sitting there as if he were dead. Perhaps he was. Selma was his widow and this man here with the blond hair had taken Josef Blau's place. Josef Blau had to do something to make them notice that he was there. He had drunk too much wine and schnapps. It didn't have to be talking, it could be something else. He could drop his cup on the floor, pull the table-cloth so that everything fell off and the coffee spilt over Herr Leopold's new brown suit. Why had he put it on? For him? For Josef Blau? Huh! He had never seen Selma before, but people talked about her, the pupils would have told him during the outing, people nudged each other in the street: That's Blau, the school-teacher who has the tall, beautiful wife, a fine figure of a woman, and they winked. Weren't Selma and Herr Leopold winking? She had pursed her lips, which she moistened with her tongue from time to time, and was smiling at the new teacher. When she took a drink of coffee, she held her arm out horizontally from her body and stuck out her little finger.

Josef Blau could not drink his coffee. It left a bitter taste in his mouth. Now Selma's mother was handing round little glasses of schnapps again.

'My niece Selma isn't drinking,' said Uncle Bobek, 'out of consideration for . . . you'll have noticed yourself.'

Selma blushed. Herr Leopold said nothing either.

'Yes, yes,' Uncle Bobek went on, 'people nowadays, they can't take much any more. Our mothers used to give birth the way we sit down at table. No one made a great fuss about it . . .' Josef Blau held his breath. What was going to come next? He fixed his eyes on Uncle Bobek. Herr Leopold interrupted Uncle Bobek.

'Come now, Herr Bobek, it's easy to succumb to the temptation to play off the past against the present. I think the present times are good, and the men and women of today. Do you agree with me, Frau Blau, or are you unhappy with your contemporaries, like Herr Bobek?'

Selma laughed. They were talking as if Josef Blau were not there. He had to say something. The thoughts were going round and round in his head. Herr Leopold had rushed to Selma's aid when Uncle Bobek had started talking about giving birth. Perhaps she had given him a look. Already she was turning to him. He had saved her. Oh, Josef Blau had noticed that. They were getting closer and closer, everyone there knew it. He had to come between them, while there was still time. He could see Selma beside Herr Leopold, naked, her blond hair undone. Or perhaps he should let things take their course. She would arise, like the girl in that book, only he couldn't remember her name – what was she called now? – and follow him, mute and refusing to be turned away. But he was still alive, he opened his mouth, they had forgotten him but they were about to hear from him.

'Let's do some gymnastics,' he said.

It wasn't what he meant to say. It was stupid. He should have said something else. How did that get into his head? His mind was confused, no doubt about it. Herr Leopold gave him a nod. Bobek refilled the glasses with schnapps. His hand was trembling and he soiled the table-cloth.

'You're right,' said Herr Leopold. 'For too long we have neglected our bodies. People are starting to value healthy and well-formed bodies once again. I am a member of the gymnastic association.'

He leant back. Selma did not take her eyes off him. Uncle

69

Bobek had got up from his chair and was cautiously man-
oeuvring his way towards the sofa.

'You must give your body what it needs,' the new teacher
went on. 'Exercise it, expose it to the fresh air, the sunshine, let
it be naked as much as possible.'

'Ooh, you!' Selma's mother screamed.

'I'm serious. We all have bodies, just as we have minds,
that's the way we are. We shouldn't be ashamed of them. I'm
sure all this sounds very stupid to you, Frau Blau?'

He said it to Selma as if the two of them were alone
together. As if there was no one in the room. Not Uncle
Bobek, wheezing as he twisted and turned on the sofa, eyes
closed; not Selma's mother, nor even him, Josef Blau.

Selma had red blotches on her cheeks. Her breast heaved
with every breath. She did not reply, since out of Uncle
Bobek's mouth came a long-drawn-out noise from the very
depths of his body. Uncle Bobek waved his right hand apolo-
getically. 'Pardon me,' he said. 'Frailty thy name is humanity.
When you get to my age you can't hold things back any more.
It was a new wine, Mathilda dear.'

Herr Leopold stood up. He kissed Selma's hand. Uncle
Bobek had closed his eyes again. Selma's mother was going to
tug his sleeve, but Herr Leopold restrained her.

Chapter Six

Uncle Bobek was fast asleep. It was impossible to wake him to bed him down on the sofa. Selma's mother tried to shift his body into a more comfortable position, but it proved beyond her.

Selma had opened the window.

'Fresh air,' said Josef Blau.

She did not understand. She nodded at him, as if she was pleased to have guessed what he wanted.

If Uncle Bobek had not emitted that animal noise, perhaps Josef Blau would have come out on top and Selma would have looked at him full of admiration. He had had a quick-witted reply on the tip of his tongue when it happened. 'This must all sound very stupid to you, Frau Blau,' Herr Leopold had said, looking at Selma. What if Josef Blau had given him the answer that was already forming on his lips? He was too long making up his mind. But if Uncle Bobek could have held himself back, Josef Blau would have said, 'It sounds the way it is.' He would have said it calmly, without the least agitation, continuing to stare into space, as if he were not present.

It seemed a clever and dignified reply to him. It would have crushed Herr Leopold. He would make a note of it, look at it again in the morning when his head was clear. He must think all this through in the morning. His brain was too tired now. He wanted to go to bed. He was thinking of everything at once, there was no order in his mind.

He heard Karpel singing in the forest in front of him, very loud, as someone out walking might do from fear. What kind of reception would he get from the class? Selma and the new teacher, God, the way one tempted fate, Uncle Bobek making him look ridiculous – what had he used the money for? Josef Blau could not focus on any of it, one thing blurred into another.

He was lying in bed, stretched out on his back. Selma came in. She was carrying a candle. The light flickered. Her hair shimmered as the light fell on it. She went to the cupboard. She took out a package wrapped up in paper. She unfolded a petticoat. Josef Blau recognised it. It was a lacy petticoat in pink silk such as her mother had. Selma looked at it and felt it. Then, as if she had made a sudden decision, she threw off her clothes. For a moment she stood naked in the flickering candlelight. Then she put the petticoat on. It stretched tight over her belly, but around her breasts and under her arms it formed delicate folds. She looked at herself in the mirror.

'He's a fool,' Josef Blau said.

She whirled round. Had she thought he was asleep?

'It's not my fault,' she said, taking off the petticoat, carefully folding it and putting it back in the cupboard. 'He arrived with some meat and asked us to cook it. He ordered Martha to fetch some wine. Who could imagine we'd have a visitor?

Did she deliberately not understand whom he was talking about?

'How long have you known him?' he asked. 'You've known him for a long time. Go on, you can tell me.'

'Who?'

'Herr Leopold, the gymnast, hahaha. He was doing gymnastics naked with the boys in the meadow. He's a fool, you know, him and his muscular chest?'

'Don't talk like that,' she said. 'You've been drinking. Get some sleep.'

'Yes, I've been drinking. I'm not used to it. But I'm sober, soberer than sober . . . it's bright and clear inside my head . . . a painful light . . . I can see everything . . . everything is so clear I could touch it, but I'm not stretching out my hand, see . . . I don't want to stretch it out, or I'm afraid to . . . or nothing matters any more, Selma . . . I could talk about everything, say everything . . . It's as if my body were raised up and floating, without having to hold on. I'm lying down, but I can't feel the bed. I'm holding onto the bed with my hands, but I can't feel it. Everything's a long way away . . . all the horrors, I can observe them . . . Perhaps everything will be all right, yes, yes . . . My thoughts are all tangled up together, but still each individual one is clear. This cannot turn out all right in the end, I say, but I'm not praying, it makes no difference one way or the other, I say, things will take their course. When Herr Leopold left, didn't someone – who was it now? – say, "A charming man." It was your mother. Everyone's against me. They'll drive you towards him, like beaters at a hunt, whether you want them to or not. I'll try to stand in their way, but in the end I'll be one of the beaters as well. Perhaps we can't do anything about it. Good, good, one two, one two, Uncle Bobek snores like a clock. An old man can't hold things back any more. You're laughing at me, Selma, go on, you can say it, Selma, that's all right.'

'I'm not laughing. When, like me, your time might come any day, there's only one thing on your mind.'

She put out the light.

She was only thinking about one thing. Why then had she bought a silk petticoat and why, why had she put it on, today of all days, and looked at herself in the mirror? When was she thinking of wearing it? When she met him? Had they already agreed a rendezvous? Now she was asleep. Josef Blau kept his eyes open. It was difficult, but whenever he closed them for a few seconds, he felt as if he were standing on a swaying surface with nothing to hold on to. He lost his sense of where he was, however much he reminded himself he was in a horizontal position, lying stretched out on his bed. He could not remember where his head was, felt it far down below, up above, hanging underneath his legs, sending the blood rushing to it. He sat up in bed and listened. Selma's mother was turning over and over in bed. The regularity of Uncle Bobek's snores as he breathed in and out was unbearable.

There was no escape, you could not avoid it, even if you pulled the blanket over your head or stuck your fingers in your ears. What did Uncle Bobek need the money for?

Selma was sleeping soundly. Should he strike a match to see if she was smiling? Perhaps her dream was written all over her face and he would be able to read it. Perhaps he would see that she was dreaming of Herr Leopold. He could wake her, tell her what he had seen and she would not dare deny it. Was she dreaming that she was lying in bed beside the new teacher? He was broad-shouldered and full of strength. Beside him she would not be condemned to wither, as she was beside Josef Blau. Herr Leopold would wrap his arms around her, so tight that she cried out. She was filled with desire like him, as he leant over her and took her. There was no defence against Herr Leopold, she was in a hurry to join him, in her dream and in her daytime existence, they had all sensed it and no one had dared question the pair of them. A charming man, Selma's mother had said. Herr Leopold had looked at Selma, calmly, in the eyes, shamelessly, as if she were already his wife, while he, Josef Blau, sat in the background. No one paid him any attention, they turned to the other, to the victor. Josef Blau was dead, forgotten. Herr Leopold had heard what the boys called out behind Blau's back, perhaps he was telling her as she sat on his lap in her lacy silk petticoat, and they laughed and kept repeating it to each other. 'Theresa.' He was not going to allow it, he was going to stop it. He was going to stand in their way, find out their secrets, watch their every breath. If Selma's long dress was no protection, he would not hesitate to demand the next step, it had already been on the tip of his tongue. She must cut off her thick blond hair, so that her head was as bald as a nun's. Like that she could not become a man's mistress, not with her head shaven bare.

He was going to talk to Uncle Bobek. Today he could say everything. He wanted to know. About the money and how much more virile than he Herr Leopold might be. Uncle Bobek must know that. Cautiously Josef Blau got out of bed, legs first so that it would not creak. He felt his way along the wall. Selma had left the wardrobe door open, Josef Blau's hand caught it. The door creaked. Selma stirred. Josef Blau stood still. He held his breath. Now she was sound asleep again.

He opened the living-room door, went in and closed it slowly. It didn't creak. He smiled. He had taken the greatest possible care, had opened the door so slowly that anyone watching would hardly have noticed it moving. How long had he taken, first his legs, then going to the door, opening it, closing it? An hour perhaps, perhaps two. He had not lost patience. Now the door was closed. Uncle Bobek would cry out when he woke him. He lit the lamp and held it up, shining it in Uncle Bobek's face. Perhaps Uncle Bobek would slip from his deep sleep into a light slumber. Then he would be easier to wake. Uncle Bobek's snores continued undiminished. His head had fallen back, his mouth was wide open, revealing the black stumps of his teeth.

The bottle of kümmel was on the table. Josef Blau picked it up and poured some schnapps into a tumbler. Then he sat down beside Uncle Bobek, the glass in his hand.

It was cold. The window was still open. It's strange, thought Josef Blau. Even if the days are as warm as in summer, spring nights are cool. Everything else is the same. The air and the ground warm up in the sun. The temperature today was a summer temperature. Why was the night colder than a summer's night? How was it that the air and the earth's crust cooled down more quickly in springtime than in the summer? That was all beside the point. He hadn't got out of bed and come to sit freezing in his nightshirt beside Uncle Bobek, with a tumbler of schnapps in his hand, in order to ruminate on that. He wanted to ask him two questions, clear questions: about the new teacher and about the money. But still it was strange. He'd try to find the answer in the morning, when his head had stopped aching. He said it out loud, so as not to forget it: the cooling of the earth's crust. You needed to protect yourself. The cooling was greater than he had at first supposed. His legs were shivering. They were encased in long white trousers tied together at the ankles. He put the glass down on the table and went over to close the window. There was a voluminous article of clothing hanging over the back of a chair. He pulled the sleeves on. It came down to his calves. Josef Blau picked up the tumbler of schnapps and sat down beside Uncle Bobek,

He started by stroking Bobek's hand, which was lying on the sofa. Then he gave him a cautious prod. Uncle Bobek did not wake up. He gave him a more vigorous prod, shook his shoulder. When that did not work, Josef Blau stood up. He held the glass over the sleeping man, then tipped it to pour the schnapps into his open mouth. Uncle Bobek shot up, sending the schnapps spilling all over his waistcoat. He gasped for breath, flailed his arms around, opened his eyes, snorted and then began to cough convulsively. Josef Blau watched him in horror. His bloodshot eyes were almost popping out, his head straining forward with the effort. It looked as if he was going to choke. He pressed his hands to his heart and stared fixedly at Josef Blau. Josef Blau dropped the glass. What had he done? Uncle Bobek made a sign with his hands. Josef Blau understood. He went behind him and thumped him with his fist on his broad back.

The coughing subsided. Uncle Bobek gestured to Josef Blau to stop. Then he leant back. He was breathing regularly, even if it was an effort.

'Drink!' said Uncle Bobek in a dry voice.

Josef Blau picked up the tumbler from the floor, filled it half full and handed it to Bobek. Bobek drank. He took a deep breath.

'A piece of luck you were here.' He spoke so quietly Josef Blau could hardly understand what he said. 'Without you I'd have choked to death. Sit down.'

Josef Blau sat down beside him. Bobek looked him up and down. Then he smiled and patted him on the shoulder with his fat hand.

'Bring me something to eat,' he said.

Josef Blau could see nothing to eat in the room. He took the lamp and went into the kitchen. He found some bones and chunks of meat on a plate, found a knife and fork and cut a few slices of bread. Then he looked for a napkin. Uncle Bobek, who was sitting in the dark, began to get impatient.

'Over here, my child,' he said as Josef Blau came in.

Josef Blau pulled a chair over to the sofa and placed the things he had brought on it in front of Bobek.

Uncle Bobek didn't bother with the knife and fork. He picked up the chunks of meat in his short, fat fingers and stuffed them in his mouth. From time to time he lubricated his throat with a drink from the tumbler Josef Blau was holding.

'Almost went to meet my Maker there,' said Uncle Bobek. 'You see how quickly it could all be over. Do you believe in God?'

Josef Blau said nothing.

'You're an educated man, do you believe in God?'

'Oh, I do,' said Josef Blau.

'I'm a good Christian.' Uncle Bobek leant over to Josef Blau and placed his arm round his shoulders. Josef Blau sat bolt upright. 'A good Roman Catholic Christian. Don't let me hear anyone say a word against it, my child, or I'll give them a piece of my mind that'll leave them flat on the floor. And they won't get up that quickly either. I've stuck to everything it says in the Catechism, haven't I, my child?'

Josef Blau nodded his head. Bobek looked at him.

'Have I not gone to confession and communion as often as the next man? You see. No one can make any accusations against me and there will be saints to intercede for me, don't you think?'

Uncle Bobek sat there, unmoving, his arm round Josef Blau.

'A boozer, a glutton, a belly like a barrel, you say? A man like that can't go to heaven? Hey, now you tell me something, why – you're an educated man, that's why I'm asking you – why are the saints all so skinny and scrawny and look like something from the seven lean years? Why are there no fat ones among them, no plump ones with a warm belly and round cheeks. It's an injustice, I tell you, it's not right, that's my opinion. Have there been no fat martyrs for the faith? Look at me, my child. It's a great injustice, it's enough to drive you to despair.' The tears ran down Uncle Bobek's cheeks and into his moustache.

'That's the trouble with God.' He took a drink from the glass and calmed down. 'Bobek has no confidence in Him. How could he have, under the circumstances? You'll grant me that, won't you?'

Josef Blau did not answer. What was there he could say? He was looking for an opportunity to ask Uncle Bobek questions, but Bobek went on talking.

'I believe everything and stick to everything it says in the Catechism, don't you see? But just a minute. There's this one problem with God, a point where I can't go along with it any more. I have no confidence, I tell you. You see, He despises fat people because they stuff themselves, fat people are not liked. What should I do about that? Take it lying down, you think? God forgive me, you never know when you're going to meet your Maker, but I'm not going to take it lying down, I can tell you. I refuse to believe in Him. There's nothing else I can do about it, but that, I tell you, that I can and will do. No one can rise up against me. I've stuck to everything, but on the quiet, if you see what I'm getting at. If someone doesn't like me, then I don't like them.'

He found a piece of gristly meat on a bone and started to gnaw at it.

'Can this be a sin? The pigeons, they fly about, they pick up the seeds from the ground. Do you know how many ways there are to cook a pigeon? Your Uncle Bobek knows seventeen ways, sweet and sour and spicy, stuffed and roasted. Who was it now, who was the man who invented wine?'

'Noah.'

'Noah! There you are. And who gave him the idea? God, don't you see, God who created everything, from the sun to the caraway seed. There was a man where I come from, I couldn't keep up with him when he sat down to eat. He closed his eyes at every mouthful and once we were at the inn and there was hare with gravy and dumplings and red cabbage. But there was something in the gravy – they knew how to make it where I come from – that made you rub your tongue against the roof of your mouth and squeeze the juices out of the meat between your jaws to the last drop, I've never tasted hare like that since.'

The saliva gathered in Uncle Bobek's mouth and dribbled down over his lips. 'We didn't want to stop. But then this man put his knife and fork down and closed his eyes and chewed and smacked his lips and d'you know what he did, my child, do you know what he did? "God created that," he said, "praise be unto His name." You see? And he cried. One man hears, you see, another sees and the third closes his eyes and savours. When he got old, they said he should cut down on his food because his eyes were weak, he might go blind. Do you know what he said? "I've seen enough," he said, "but not eaten enough, not by a long chalk." He was fat and God-fearing all his life through. When people have money, you see, one man will put it in the safe, another will do business and a third will go for wine and good food. Who gives to the poor? I'm surely a charitable man. You only need to tell me a sad story and it touches my heart and brings tears to my eyes. No one can step forward and bear witness against me if my turn should come, today or tomorrow.'

'You need money for that,' said Josef Blau. Now he could ask his question.

'That's right, you need money. You make debts, you see, because you want to live. Why save it? Can you take it with you? You can be called away at any moment, after you've eaten and drunk, when you're sleeping, as we saw just now, what help is money then? What you've eaten can't be inherited by someone else, every kümmel you didn't drink is lost for good, my child. I don't save it, you see, no one will get anything from me, I have no heir apart from Selma, and who is Selma? That's you, my child, my heir. When you look good, don't you see, people will lend you money. But who's going to lend money to a man who's skinny as – God forgive me – a saint? Would Berger make him a loan? He'd laugh, that's all.'

'What did you need the thousand crowns for?' Josef Blau looked at him eagerly. Uncle Bobek laughed.

'Those thousand crowns, you see, there's a hole that has to be blocked up, but you have to make another hole to do it. I've fallen into the hands of a man who wants his money on the day it's due.

"Wait, Judas," I said, "give me a month, a week, a day."

"Not one single hour," he said. "Here's the bill of exchange," he said, "and your pension's pledged as security for it."

"All right," I said, because there are still people willing to pocket a little profit, and went to see Berger. But that didn't get me anywhere, you see, and now the man has to wait after all since I've had four months' advance on my pension already. I will pay, I'll sort it out, but I need time, time, time, he'll have to learn to wait. You see, as I was going away from your house, my child, clutching the money to my breast, so to speak, what's the point of saving it, as I say, my hands started to itch and my mouth to water. A goulash and two glasses of beer, I said, and a schnapps as a nightcap. But one thing leads to another, you know, we stayed there till twelve. Then one of us got up and we all went with him to the brothel in Kasernengasse, hahaha, yes, my child, your Uncle Bobek's still got what it takes.'

So he went to Kasernengasse at night as well, like Modlizki and Karpel. They might even have met there, Karpel and Bobek, and Karpel had told Uncle Bobek things and that was why he was smiling like that just now.

'Did you meet anyone you knew there?' Josef Blau asked, his eyes fixed on the flickering candle flame.

'Naturally. You meet the odd fellow there who goes round with his eyes fixed on the ground during the day.'

'Karpel, was there one called that?'

'Karpel? Karpel?' Bobek's head swayed from side to side as he thought. 'No one gives his name there unless he has to. Quite possible I know him. They all know me. I'm not embarrassed, you see, being a widower. What should I do with it, let it go to waste? They all shout "Uncle Bobek!" when I arrive, the girls and the customers, just like you and Selma. But I say, "Don't call me uncle," I say, "I'm a match for any twenty-year-old," I say.'

Josef Blau pricked up his ears. 'For twenty-year-olds?'

'You doubt my word? No one's dared say that before. What did I say just now? My heir I called you, and now this! Right then, get your trousers on, they'll still let us in. If you come with me they'll let us in. I'll call the madam, Fritzi's her name, I knew her when she was just one of the girls. I'll show you what I'm made of, even after all the wine and schnapps. You think that has any effect on your Uncle Bobek? Not on your life, my lad. Uncle Bobek can take it. There are five girls, each

80

one prettier than the last. We won't waste any time, lad, we'll take the five all at once, no messing about downstairs, you won't have to put a coin in the music box, your Uncle Bobek doesn't need a musical accompaniment. Get dressed and let's go.'

'No, no,' said Josef Blau. Bobek was pulling him by the hand, Josef Blau tried to free himself. How could he get out of it? Was Uncle Bobek really going to force him to go to Kasernengasse, now, in the night? He might meet Karpel there with Modlizki, or one of the others. It was impossible, it would be the end.

'All five of them, I say, and the madam as an encore. Is that enough for you? After all, I'm tired. Do you believe me? Do you believe me, now? Tell me straight, and no excuses.'

Bobek thrust his head forward and looked him in the eye. He still had hold of his hand.

'Yes, yes,' said Josef Blau.

Bobek let go.

'I'm not as young as I used to be,' Uncle Bobek went on, after a pause. He gave a melancholy nod. 'There's no denying it. No, no. You should have seen me when I was twenty, thirty. And still at forty. Now it's the turn of others, the younger generation, people like you, eh?'

Josef Blau was horrified, What did Uncle Bobek want of him?

'Though I wouldn't say you were the strongest of men, eh? Hahaha! I wouldn't mind asking Selma, in strict confidence, of course.'

Josef Blau felt the blood rush to his head. 'Stop it,' he said.

'Now, now, don't worry, I'm not going to. I wouldn't want to embarrass the girl anyway, hahaha. But she might not even know it can be different, with a real man . . .'

'Uncle!'

'Uncle! Uncle! Don't worry, I'm not saying anything. Wouldn't dream of it. Be sent away with a flea in my ear, most likely. But a real man, you know, when I was your age and I came home at night, didn't matter how much I'd eaten or drunk, didn't even bother to take the cigar out of my mouth,

81

day in, day out, year after year, it made no difference what Martha said, God rest her soul, I wouldn't take no for an answer. And that wasn't everything that was going on. Just look about you in the neighbourhood and you'll see them running round, must be thirty little Bobeks at least. Sometimes cost me a pretty penny, but why save it, I always say.'

Josef Blau stood up. 'That's all lies,' he said.

'Hahaha, you think I'm lying because I'm not like you. Not one of your scrawny, dried-out saints, God forgive me. But what's the point in holding back. There's more I could say. Someone who's young and a man can do all sorts of things, someone like that new teacher, what was his name, now . . .?'

Josef Blau stared at Bobek. He raised his hands as if he were going to throttle him, the blood was throbbing in the veins of his neck. The room was going up and down. Was it because the candle was flickering and the shadows dancing on the walls, or was it still the wine that had gone to his head?

Uncle Bobek fell silent.

'Lies!' said Josef Blau. 'All lies!'

Uncle Bobek said nothing.

'Tell me you're lying,' Josef Blau shouted.

Bobek looked at him but did not reply.

'And what about the money? I'm asking you!' Josef Blau panted. 'It's all going down your throat or into your belly. You'll ruin us all. I want the money, d'you hear! Tell me, how are you going to give me the money when the time comes? Out with it. Or . . . or . . .'

He took a step towards him.

'Don't raise your hand to me,' said Uncle Bobek, shifting sideways along the sofa in his attempt to get out of the way.

'Tell me!'

'The money will be there.'

'Where will you get it?'

'If there's no other way, I'll marry our dear Mathilda.' Uncle Bobek sighed.

The candle flickered. Someone had opened the door quietly.

Josef Blau turned round. He saw Selma. She had thrown a coat over her shoulders. 'What's going on?' she asked.

'Nothing, nothing,' said Uncle Bobek. 'We're just having a little chat.'

'Oh,' said Selma, 'Just look at you, hahaha. What's that you've got on?'

Josef Blau looked down. He had one of Selma's mother's voluminous dressing gowns draped over him. It was made of blue cotton with a pattern of large yellow flowers.

Selma laughed. He could still hear her after she had closed the bedroom door behind her.

Chapter Seven

During the breaks Herr Leopold was surrounded by the boys of Josef Blau's class. As always, Josef Blau stood in his place at the end of the corridor onto which the classroom doors opened. He could hear Herr Leopold's loud voice and the boys' laughter.

Nothing happened during the classes. Karpel avoided his eye, did not look up from his desk. When he was called on to answer a question, he did so with his head turned to one side.

During one of the breaks Herr Leopold went up to Josef Blau. He asked how Selma was. Josef Blau's reply was brief. He did not invite the new teacher to visit him again.

On his way home Josef Blau saw Karpel and Laub in front of him with a man dressed in black. He recognised Modlizki. Something special must be happening if Modlizki came to fetch the boys from school. He would have to go and visit him.

When he got home the next day, later than usual because of a staff meeting, Selma told him Modlizki had been there wanting to speak to him. He had not said what it was about. Without doubt important things were afoot. It was too late to go and see Modlizki that day, Josef Blau would have to put it off to the next. There was definitely something brewing. Perhaps when he was drunk Josef Blau had, by word or gesture, set in motion the thing which was now about to come to pass. He made a great effort to recall everything that had happened that night, but most of it was submerged in a loud babble of voices. He knew – and his blood turned to ice at the thought – that during that night he had lost the notion of responsibility. That notion had been something outside him, not frightening, something he could observe calmly, as if it did not concern him. He knew that he had threatened Uncle Bobek and that Herr Leopold had looked at Selma as if Josef Blau had not been there, or was dead, and he could hear Selma's laughter at the end through the closed bedroom door.

But he must not give up hope, in spite of everything. In spite of everything he must try, by the power of thought and invocation, to reach the place where fates were decided, his, Selma's and that of the child that was still to be born. Everything was linked, words, deeds and people. There was a place where they came together and that was where life and death were decided.

He would go and see Modlizki the next day, in the afternoon, that was the best time to see him. During the night he went over in his mind the questions he was going to ask him about the plans of the boys and Herr Leopold. Modlizki would look at him, head on one side, and talk. They were strange things Modlizki had to tell, even if they were ridiculous, limited in a certain sense. Perhaps all Modlizki lacked was a thorough education, but Modlizki refused to educate himself. He wanted nothing from the others, not even their knowledge. He hated them. He hated Josef Blau, even though Josef Blau was the son of a court usher who possessed no more than a man who worked at a lathe. But that was not the point, what mattered was that Josef Blau went along with the others, with good manners, refinement, what Modlizki called all that fuss and bother. Why did Modlizki always go on about his father, who had fallen off a ladder and died? Josef Blau knew about it already, he had even been there himself, drawn by the noise of the people, when Modlizki's father had been carried to the hospital. Was Modlizki trying to remind Josef Blau of his own father, who stepped off the pavement and into the street whenever the district judge came by? Josef Blau's father was tall and broad-shouldered and had a full beard, shaved clean round the chin. His cheeks were like red apples. He held himself ramrod straight, like a soldier, to the day he died. The district judge used to send him out to fetch sausages and beer.

'Just nip out and fetch me some sausages, Blau,' Wünsche, the district judge, would say.

The usher told his son about it with a loud, angry laugh. It wasn't the fact that Wünsche sent him to fetch sausages that he found insulting, it was the phrase 'just nip out'. It was as if there were something especially insulting about it beside which the other affront – that he called him 'Blau', simply Blau and not Herr Blau as befitted a man of his experience who was old enough to be the judge's father – paled into insignificance.

At five o'clock in the morning Selma stirred. Was she having a bad dream? She sat up in bed.

'Are you asleep?' she asked. 'I think it's starting.'

He leapt out of bed and quickly put on his trousers and jacket. Selma was groaning softly. She had closed her eyes. When she opened them, he was standing in the middle of the room, looking at her.

'Fetch mother,' she said.

Selma's mother was in bed. Her hair was smoothed back over her head and had large bald patches at the crown.

Josef Blau woke her up. 'It's started,' he shouted.

She got up. She stood before him in a black petticoat and a white jacket with a red pattern on the collar which hung down over her stomach.

She rushed into Selma's room and leant down over her daughter's bed. 'The contractions,' she shouted.

Josef Blau gave a start. That must have been audible in every room in the building.

Selma's mother had put on her dressing gown with the pattern of large yellow flowers. Josef Blau looked away.

'Don't stand there doing nothing,' she cried. 'Call Martha and tell her to fetch the midwife.

Josef Blau rushed down the stairs. He knocked on a door in the basement. Martha opened. All she was wearing was a skirt and a sleeveless vest. She had plaited her hair in a thin pigtail which stood out stiffly from her head like a rat's tail. Her feet were bare.

'Put your stockings on, Martha,' he said.

Martha gave him an astonished look.

'It's started,' he said. 'Fetch the midwife.'

Back upstairs he sat by the window and waited. He could hear Selma's mother walking up and down in the neighbouring room and clattering dishes. She came in. She had rolled the sleeves of her dressing gown up to the elbows. Now

Josef Blau could hear her in the kitchen. He went to the door to Selma's room. She had her eyes closed. Her mouth was open, as always, but there were lines round her lips that were unfamiliar. She seemed alien to him, as if it were the first time he had seen her. He went over to the bed. There were beads of sweat on her brow. Her breathing was irregular. Her face was distorted, ugly. Was this woman lying before him the Selma who was always the same, with the smooth, unruffled brow? Or was it a different, unknown woman?

'Selma,' he said quietly.

She was not asleep, but she did not hear him.

She had removed herself from them all, she was alone. In order to accomplish something alien, unknown, she had become alien and unknown.

Josef Blau heard steps and voices. He left the room.

The midwife came in with Martha. She was called Frau Nowak. She was grey-haired, tall and strong with a fat, round belly. On her head she had a white cap. She took a white coat out of her bag and put it on. Martha brought some warm water. Frau Nowak washed her hands carefully. Josef Blau had sat down and was writing a letter to the principal. He gave it to Martha and asked her to hand it to the school janitor. The janitor would be at the school gate at eight o'clock. She was to say nothing and answer no questions, simply hand over the letter and come back.

Meanwhile Selma's mother had brought coffee from the kitchen. She and the midwife sat down at the table. Josef Blau did not drink. He was listening. Low moans came from Selma's room. Frau Nowak looked at him.

'It's nothing,' she said. She had false teeth, her tongue pushed against them as she spoke. 'There's still a long way to go.'

The two women got up from the coffee table and went to Selma's room. Josef Blau followed them.

'Good morning, Frau Blau, dear,' said Frau Nowak, 'it's on its way, is it? Patience, patience, I always say, That's the most important thing.'

'I'm so afraid,' said Selma.

'Everything will be fine,' her mother shouted.

'She's wrestling with death,' Josef Blau thought. He had gone back into the living-room. The midwife had started to examine Selma.

'She's wrestling with death.' He clenched his fists in his pockets, determined to concentrate all his thoughts on one thing alone: that she escape death, that he should tear her away from the jaws of death. Now she was alone with the two women, but perhaps her eye was searching for him. She was demanding help from him. He had brought it upon her. If she died, he would have killed her.

Selma groaned. They held her legs and placed their hands on her body. He heard her mother's voice drowning out Selma's cries.

'Labour pains!' she screamed, making Josef Blau blush. In that voice she could just have well been saying, 'She's dead!' Why could she not speak quietly? He stood there, holding his breath so as not to create any confusion, not even through his breathing. The powers of life and death were wrestling with each other in Selma's room. Was her mother's deafness stronger than our innate fear of this moment? Selma's mother was standing there with her sleeves rolled up, neither hearing nor understanding. She was ready to help with her strong hands, placing them on the body as it tossed and turned, to soothe its convulsions, and her voice drove the invisible powers from the room. Her voice went through the doors and walls into their neighbours' apartments. She was connecting what was happening here with everyone, with the everyday lives they led, with their fate, with the thoughts, words, wishes and curses they uttered as they looked up from their coffee, from the shoes they were cleaning, from the call of nature they happened to be answering. She linked the life that was yet to be born and that he wanted to preserve to all of that, exposing it to fate and guilt.

Martha came back. She had seen the janitor at the school gate and given him the letter. He had not asked who it was from. She had not spoken to anyone. Herr Leopold will take over the class, Josef Blau thought. He will conduct the lessons in his own way, allow the boys freedoms Josef Blau denied them, destroy the discipline he had carefully built up, perhaps making it impossible to restore. He was a young teacher who did not realise what he was doing. He did not know that the boys sitting facing him were looking for any chink in his armour, were cruel, arrogant, despising the profession of those who taught them as a profession for the sons of the poor.

Tomorrow, when Josef Blau returned, the class would be strengthened in their will to resist him, their plans would have become bolder. He had not prepared himself for the encounter. He could not leave the apartment today to go and see Modlizki. He had to stay there, forget about everything, shut out everything and allow no thought into his mind but Selma.

It had gone quiet in Selma's room. Now the door opened softly. Her mother and Frau Nowak came out. Martha stayed with the mother-to-be. The two women sat down at the table again.

'You need to keep up your strength, Frau Nowak,' said Selma's mother, pouring her another cup of coffee, 'even if the coffee is cold.'

'The first child,' said Frau Nowak, pressing her tongue against her teeth, 'the first child's always a bit tricky.'

'It takes strength.'

'But she's already sweating, is our young woman. That's the main thing, believe me, I'm an experienced midwife. A good sweat, that's the main thing.'

'If labour starts before ten o'clock,' said Selma's mother, 'it'll be a boy.'

'That's just superstition.' Frau Nowak waved her hand in a dismissive gesture.

'It's what my mother used to say, God rest her soul. There were eleven of us. Four died at birth and three as infants. My mother knew what she was talking about.'

'We have to combat superstition a lot, even among people you'd expect to be experienced.'

'When do you think it'll arrive, Frau Nowak?'

'Before the evening. When the opening's the size of a thaler, the child will arrive before evening.'

'Is that for sure?'

'That's not superstition, my dear,' said Frau Nowak, offended. 'I'm an experienced midwife. There's many a doctor's had to call me in when he didn't know what to do next, my dear.'

'Selma made a vow to the Madonna of Wranau.'

'That's good, very good,' said Frau Nowak. 'Though for myself I'd have recommended the one at Bystritz. In my experience she's always given satisfaction. In hopeless cases, my dear.'

'Do you think we should . . .'

'No hurry. There'll be plenty of time for that, if need be. We mustn't rush things.'

Frau Nowak got up and opened the door to Selma's room.

'She's shut her eyes,' she said, sitting down again.

'One thing that's important, very important, is that nothing should be taken out of the room where the woman is. Not under any circumstances. I'm very strict about that. You've told the maid, I assume?'

'Nothing taken out?'

'Tell the maid. Nothing must be brought out, not a chair, not a pot, not even a cloth. Under no circumstances.'

'Should we not call a doctor?' Josef Blau asked.

Frau Nowak looked Josef Blau up and down. 'Go ahead, if you want, I've no objection. But you have to realise the doctor will throw everything off the bed, all the blankets and pillows. There'll be no more sweating after that. The sweat brings out the juices, you see, that's important. Even Doctor Frankfurter – I've worked with him for ages, an old gentleman, very amenable – even he's against sweating. But I must insist you call a doctor if you have no confidence in me.'

'No, no,' said Josef Blau, 'I have confidence.'

Selma bean to groan again.

'You stay here,' Frau Nowak said to Selma's mother. 'I'll go by myself. I'll call if I need help.'

She went to Selma. Her mother took the cups and saucers back into the kitchen.

At twelve Selma's mother brought lunch. Josef Blau did not touch it. He sat by the window, listening to the sounds coming from Selma's room, the sighs, shouts, the creaking of the bed and the midwife's constant prattle. Again and again, whenever a loud cry came to him, he would start and half get up to dash in to her, to help her. But immediately the cry died away, turned into quiet moaning and sobbing. Then even that was silent. He listened. What was that? The blood drained from his cheeks. What he feared must not come into his thoughts, for the thought might call it down. Then he heard movement again. He leant his head back and closed his eyes.

The midwife emerged from the room. 'Just a drop of soup,' she said, 'the rest can wait till after.'

Her face was red, her hair stuck to her forehead, damp with sweat. 'It'll all be over quickly. Very quickly for a first child. And everything's all right. Couldn't be better.'

At three o'clock in the afternoon Selma's mother was called into Selma's room. Martha came out, fetched some water, looked for something, then disappeared again. Josef Blau heard Selma cry out, short cries that broke off. He stood up. He was leaning forward, his hands pressed tightly together. Couldn't be better, the midwife had said. Did that mean he could hope? Was hope not presumption?

Selma started to speak, crying out, incomprehensible. That voice was not Selma's voice, it sounded like the voice of a madwoman. He listened. At first he could not make out what she was saying, but then he heard that she was praying. The litany, the invocation of the saints, endlessly repetitive, piercing, with no lowering of the voice, ending in a long-drawn-out, wild cry. Then it was quiet. Pray, he thought, help Selma's prayer, take it up. He began in a low voice, his eyes fixed on one point, with appellations of the All-high he was familiar with, then proceeding to unusual, unknown ones, which would be heard, straining with all his might to find the one word, the word of release, of liberation.

The door opened and Frau Nowak came in. She found him standing there, moving his lips, blind to what was going on around him. It was five o'clock.

She grasped his hand. 'Come,' she said.

She pulled him along, unresisting. They went into Selma's room. Selma smiled at him. She whispered something, but he could not understand what it was. Her face was smooth, with no trace of the lines that had transformed it earlier. It seemed different now, gentler, even though it was a tired face, more expressive. He leant over her. Then the midwife drew him to one side and pointed to a white bundle of pillows in a basket on a chair beside the bed. Selma's eyes followed him as he looked at it. He saw a tiny, red, wrinkled face with its eyes shut.

Selma tried to speak. The midwife put a finger to her lips.

'A boy,' said Frau Nowak.

At that moment the boy opened his eyes. They were staring fixedly at Josef Blau. Then he opened his mouth and emitted a feeble, long-drawn-out noise that sounded like a pathetic croak.

Selma gave a tired smile.

The midwife took Josef Blau by the hand and led him back into the living-room. 'Right,' she said, 'now let her sleep.'

'She's alive!' thought Josef Blau. 'She's alive!'

The tiny thing lying next to her was his son. 'My son,' he said softly, to make it sink in that something special had come into his life. He heard the two women eating and drinking. Selma's mother called to him to join them. He shook his head. 'My son,' he thought, and, 'She's alive, she's sleeping.'

'What did I say, Frau Nowak?' Selma's mother said. 'If labour starts before ten it'll be a boy.'

'A coincidence,' said Frau Nowak. 'But we managed without a doctor, as you can see.' She looked at Josef Blau.

'Thank you,' he said.

'And it's a son I brought you as well. Yes, yes. You're in good hands with Frau Nowak, that's what they all say. Congratulations, Herr Professor.' She went up to Josef Blau and held out her hand.

'A strong, healthy baby. God's blessing be on him,' she said.

'Touch wood,' shouted Selma's mother, rapping the table-top with her knuckles.

'And what's he going to be christened?' asked Frau Nowak.

'Josef Albert,' Selma's mother shouted. 'His Uncle Bobek will be his godfather, Albert Bobek.'

'Oh, Herr Bobek! He's chosen a good godfather there. Such a nice man, such a good man is Herr Bobek.'

So the wrinkled infant with the old man's face and the pathetic croak in the next room would have a name, would be a specific individual. Josef Albert Blau. Josef Blau had not thought of that before. That alone would distinguish him from all other people, from old Hämisch, who lived in the same building, from Modlizki, from Uncle Bobek, the fact that he had a particular name, a name that was bound to him, and he to it. That name would make him an individual. He lay there and croaked and slept. And you gave him a name. You selected one, Martin or Franz, whichever you happened to like, the name of the saint on whose day he was born, his godfather's name, his father's name. Who had determined it? Was the name nothing? Did the name not have its own fate? By giving him a name you marked out the new-born child for the first time, after you had given him life, put him at the mercy of an unknown, unfathomable fate, that he would have to endure. Josef like his father and Albert like his uncle, the two men to whom he was so closely linked. Would he survive as Josef Albert? Perhaps he would have been a different person with a different name and a different godfather, just as he would surely have been a different person with a different father. Should Josef Blau rise up and say, 'According to the teachings of our church there is a spiritual bond between godfather and godchild, comparable to the bond between father and son. I do not want Uncle Bobek to be his godfather.' But who could he propose, which name, which godfather? Could he know that the other man was better? Was it not better to let things be, not to intervene, not to change anything, not to call anything down on him, not to set anything in motion?

There was a knock at the door. Martha opened it. Uncle Bobek came in, gasping for breath. He collapsed on the sofa before he spoke. First of all he nodded to everyone.

'Well done,' he said, wheezing. 'Congratulations. What is it, actually?'

'A boy,' Selma's mother shouted.

'I've got to hand it to you, Blau,' Bobek said, 'I didn't think you had it in you. It was young Hämisch who told me. I ran into him in the street half an hour ago. "Buy a nice present for the christening," he said. "I imagine you'll be the godfather." I rushed over and up the stairs and here I am.'

So the child was bound to them all already. They were talking about it in the streets, involving and entangling it in their thoughts, conversations and relationships, in which it was now inextricably entwined.

Selma's mother had quietly gone into Selma's room. She came out with the white bundle in her arms. Carefully she drew the covering sheet aside and held the child out to Uncle Bobek.

'A magnificent specimen!' Uncle Bobek exclaimed. 'Dududu, tarrallaa, kitchikitchikoo.' He wagged his finger at the child and roared with laughter.

'Who do you think it looks like, Herr Bobek?' Frau Nowak asked.

Uncle Bobek took another look at the child. 'As God's my witness,' he said, 'he looks like my dear Mathilda.'

In the evening a messenger brought a basket of roses. There was a card among them with congratulations from Herr Leopold.

'A charming man,' said Selma's mother. She wanted to go and tell Selma right away, but Selma was asleep. When she woke up, the flowers were beside her bed. Selma looked at them and smiled.

'Those are from Herr Leopold,' said Josef Blau.

Did she not understand, or did she know?

She looked at the flowers and smiled.

Chapter Eight

That night Josef Blau slept in the living-room. Frau Nowak slept in his bed, that had been moved away from Selma's.

He heard the infant crying. Was it hungry? Its mother had not yet suckled it. It's the first night in Josef Albert's life, Josef Blau thought. Josef Albert. We're already calling him by his name.

Josef Albert cried and went back to sleep, only to wake and cry again, lustily at first, then more and more feebly until he fell silent. He went to sleep when his tiredness was greater than his hunger. He will have many more nights, Josef Blau thought, in which tiredness will eventually submerge everything – fear, worry, prayer, regret, pain – in a light, dream-tossed sleep. Josef Albert has torn himself free from his mother. He is breathing. He has a name. Inside his mother he was his mother's breath, heartbeat, hunger, pain, joy. He has been Josef Albert for ten hours and already no one knows what is inside him. Is it just the hunger crying out of him, or his fear of all the frightening things surrounding him, of the gigantic, bare, red faces with the dark, wide-open maws bending over him and emitting terrible noises – they strike Josef Albert's ear-drum like claps of thunder – of the bright light, of the cold? He was in warmth and darkness. Does he remember? Does he know? No one reaches him. He is alone. There is a gap between him and everything that he will never bridge. He has parents. The father talks to his son. What do they say? They do not understand each other. Will Josef Albert understand his father when he looks at him, speaks to him? He is Josef Blau's flesh and blood. He is his son. He has been born into his father's life, into his entanglements, into his name, into the ugly face of his deaf grandmother that he bears, born today, why not tomorrow, in ten years, in a hundred? When his son questions him, demands an explanation, will he understand his father's words, his looks, his mute embrace? Can he understand what Selma cannot: that their fates are interconnected. Will he not ask him why, why is my fate linked with yours, with Josef Blau's and not with something else? His father will not cease fighting to protect him, so that the son shall not be the victim of a fate for which his father, his mother are to blame, or even just set in motion through a word, an act.

The door to Selma's room opened. Josef Blau awoke with a start. It was Frau Nowak in a white bed-jacket, which made her body beneath it rounder, larger.

'What has happened?'

'Nothing, it's all right,' said Frau Nowak. She pronounced the 's' with a lisp, she said 'sh'. She had taken her dentures out. 'It's the flowers. The scent is too strong. I'll put them here. Everything is all right.'

The scent of the flowers was bad for the new mother and her baby. Herr Leopold's flowers had to be removed. Perhaps, when she woke up, Selma would look for the flowers and smile. Now the flowers were not there. Perhaps Selma would ask the midwife about them. But the midwife would not take them back in. Their scent was too strong, they were bad for her, they poisoned the air. No one had thought of sending flowers, only Herr Leopold had thought of it. In the morning, when the principal had instructed him to take over Herr Blau's class, he would have learnt that Selma had gone into labour. But who had told him the baby had arrived? He would not have sent the flowers if he had not known, since everything could have turned out differently.

Perhaps Herr Leopold had sent a messenger to enquire about Selma. Perhaps he had come to the house himself. He might even have posted someone to stand watch outside the house all the time, his eyes fixed on Blau's window, a pupil from Blau's class who had taken on the task. He had seen his teacher at the window, heard Selma's cries, her mother's voice. He had hurried off to report to Herr Leopold.

In his first hour Josef Albert had breathed in the scent of Herr Leopold's flowers. He did not know yet and already Herr Leopold was around him, Herr Leopold, who looked at

Josef Albert's mother as if Josef Blau had long since been forgotten. His mother had smiled when she saw the flowers. She did not ask and she smiled. Either she knew or she suspected. But everyone had known, from the moment Herr Leopold came into the room, looked at her candidly and spoke to her as if there were nothing in the way between him and her. Everyone knew, everything, even that he would send her flowers. They had a strong scent. Should he get up, open the window and throw the flowers out into the street? What did Herr Leopold want? What would be next? What now? Once it had happened, everyone would feel they had known from the beginning. Now Josef Albert was was there. Josef Blau must go to his bed, talk to him. You got a headache from the heady scent that filled the room. Josef Albert must stand by Josef Blau, who would stand in the way, throw the flowers out of the window. He would be alone with him. Selma and her mother were not there, perhaps out with Herr Leopold, just Josef Blau with his son, he put his arms round his son and said, 'Love your father, Josef Albert, come what may.'

Josef Blau came to with a start. He opened his eyes. Had he said it out loud? He felt he had heard the sound of his voice. He got up and opened the window. There were lights moving at the station. A train whistled in the distance. Someone was bawling out a song in the street.

Fresh air, thought Josef Blau.

He got back into bed. Josef Albert was crying. Selma was awake too. He heard her talking to the midwife. She'll be asking about the flowers, Josef Blau thought.

When he woke up, the midwife was warming some milk on the primus stove in his room.

'A slight temperature,' she said, 'but it's not serious. She's asked for you several times. But I wasn't to wake you.'

Josef Blau went into Selma's room. The curtains were drawn. Selma was lying on her back. In her hands she was clutching a crumpled handkerchief. Her hair was dishevelled and hanging down over her forehead. She wasn't smiling, as she had been the previous evening. Her face was flushed, her eyes moved restlessly to and fro. They were large and the fever flickered in them. It was worse than he had thought from what the midwife had said. Oh God, he had hoped the danger was over.

'We must fetch the doctor,' he said in a low voice to Frau Nowak.

The midwife made no objection. 'I'll send Martha,' she replied.

He went over to the bed. Selma tried to sit up. Then she grasped his hand and pulled him close. Her hand was hot and dry. Frau Nowak had gone out.

'Just in case,' Selma said. 'Good that I've seen you before you go.'

'Selma,' he said. He could not say any more. He held her hand and squeezed it, as if by that he could keep hold of Selma. Selma tossed and turned restlessly under the heavy eiderdown. She propped herself up on her left hand and put her lips close to his ear.

'Karpel has the bill of exchange,' she said, sinking back into the pillows.

Josef Blau let go of her hand.

'What . . . what are you saying, Selma?'

She had shut her eyes. Her breathing was loud, her breast was rising and falling unevenly. Could she not hear him? Was she asleep? Was it all over? Had she saved up all her strength to tell him that one thing before she went? She loved him! Selma loved him! She had not asked about the flowers. Ill with the fever, all she had thought for was that he should come while she could still speak so she that could warn him.

Frau Nowak came in again. 'Is she asleep?' she asked. She looked at Josef Blau. 'It's not serious. It's normal. You mustn't let yourself get worked up, Herr Professor.'

She pushed him, unresisting, out of Selma's room.

'It's nothing,' Selma's mother said as she placed his coffee on the table.

'It's nothing,' said the doctor, who came to see Selma soon after.

If it was nothing, then it was still something. At first Josef Blau had not understood. But now he saw. Karpel had the bill of exchange. He could only have bought it from Berger, the friend who had lent Bobek the money. But how did Selma come to know? Selma must confess whom she had heard it from. Who had an interest in telling Selma? Only the person who wanted Josef Blau to hear: Karpel, who wanted to keep his teacher in fear, humiliate him, use the bill of exchange to render his teacher defenceless at school. Had he ambushed Selma in the street, whispered it to her? Or did they meet, talk, had talked together at least once? Selma had hesitated to tell her husband so that he would not pester her with questions about where she had heard it. Had Josef Blau ever mentioned the name of Karpel? She had spoken it as if it were a familiar name to her, one she often heard. How had Karpel come to hear about the bill of exchange? Was that Selma too? She must tell him everything. As soon as he was allowed to see her, he would press her, nothing must remain hidden. She might perhaps never have revealed that she knew, but the fever had made her speak, the fear of death, the exhaustion from giving birth, the terrifying images the illness had brought to her drowsy brain and her worry about her new-born baby. If Selma's condition allowed, he would go and see Modlizki that very day. As long as the bill of exchange was in Karpel's hands, the teacher was at his pupil's mercy. They were unusual things Karpel was planning, frightening plans.

How had Karpel approached Selma? What pretence had he used to get her to meet him? Perhaps Karpel had long been threatening to take his revenge, to destroy the teacher, and Selma had bought him off. She must speak. They might even all know, the class, Selma's mother, Modlizki, only he did not know that he had been saved not by his prayers, but by Selma, who bought the pupils off. What was the price Selma paid? What had she done already, how far had she gone? What was Karpel asking for now as the price for not presenting Josef Blau with the bill of exchange?

Selma was sleeping now. She had taken some soup and suckled the baby for the first time. Her temperature had gone down. Her mother and Frau Nowak were in the living-room.

'There's no danger,' Frau Nowak said. He could go. It was half past seven when he left the apartment.

Herr Leopold was in the corridor, ready to stand in for Josef Blau again. He went up to Josef Blau, holding out his hand in a broad gesture.

'Heartiest congratulations. Since you're here, both must be doing well.'

Josef Blau shook his hand without a word.

He went into the classroom, as always crossing the dais, not letting the boys out of his sight as he went to his place. He hung his hat on the peg and signed the class register. All this was done very quickly. He did not want a deputation from the boys, as was usual with other teachers, to come up and congratulate him. He stood by the window and started the lesson, taking up from where he had finished the last one.

Karpel sat there like the other boys, unmoving, head bowed.

Chapter Nine

Modlizki was standing at the top of the steps, a black figure, in his high-buttoned waistcoat. He came towards Josef Blau, unhurried as always, his head with its black hair parted in the middle tilted slightly to the left.

They went into the wood-panelled hall.

Josef Blau sat down. He had his back to the window and in front of him the mounted animal heads and weapons. Modlizki stood before him. With a gesture, he invited Modlizki to sit down. Modlizki sat down at a respectful distance on the edge of a chair standing by itself. He sat upright, not leaning against the backrest.

Modlizki looked at Josef Blau expectantly. Josef Blau shifted uneasily in his chair. He had to speak first. Modlizki, he knew, would do nothing to bring the agonising silence to an end.

'You came to see me, Modlizki,' he said. 'It was not possible for me to come any sooner. There has been . . .'

'I am aware of that,' said Modlizki. He stood up. 'I would have made it my duty to express my congratulations at the earliest opportunity.'

'Thank you,' said Josef Blau. 'Sit down Modlizki.'

There was so much to discuss. Where should he begin? He had to be careful, not expose himself.

'A boy?' Modlizki asked. Josef Blau nodded. 'He will have the good fortune to enjoy a proper upbringing. That was not the case with me. My father . . .'

'I know,' said Josef Blau. Modlizki bowed and was silent.

He should not have interrupted Modlizki. Now he had to start all over again.

'Who was it who told you, Modlizki? About the baby, I mean.'

'Young Master Karpel came round yesterday. It is a habit of mine to stand outside the house in the evenings. The evenings are warm, it could almost be summer.'

'Karpel? From my class? You talked about me?'

'We talked of this and that. The young gentleman does me the honour of taking me into his confidence. I believe I took the liberty of mentioning it on a previous occasion.'

'What did he say?'

' "We had a new teacher today," he said. I asked whether Herr Blau was ill. No, the young gentleman replied, it was his wife who was knocked up, but she must have calved by now. That was the way the young gentleman expressed himself. It is not my place to admonish him. In my reply I took the liberty of emphasising that giving birth to a child is a happy event.'

Modlizki did not smile. Not a muscle moved in his face. His voice was deep and monotonous. It did not rise and fall. Josef Blau stared at the floor, at the colourful pattern of the carpet.

'The young gentleman likes strong language,' Modlizki went on. 'It could well be such as to offend sensitive ears. He has been well brought up. In my opinion it is a certain devilry that impels him to erase the effects of that upbringing. I would not be so presumptuous as to stand in judgment, but I do not doubt that the young gentleman will cause a stir at some point.'

'When?' Josef Blau asked.

'That I could not say. I did not have anything specific in mind, my intention was to talk in general terms.'

'You think he is someone out of the ordinary, Modlizki?'

'That is what I wanted to indicate, in general terms.'

'For good or evil?'

'I do not know. What I do know is that he will do something exceptional. Perhaps some will find it good, others evil. I think that could be what will happen.'

'I think there is a dividing line between good and evil. There are also things that lie between them. But . . . surely one can tell whether something exceptional, something out of the ordinary is one thing or the other?'

Modlizki looked at Josef Blau. Josef Blau had not put it well. The way Modlizki was looking at him made him uncertain. Modlizki was waiting.

'Go on, tell me, Modlizki,' said Josef Blau.

'I have not had the advantage of an education, I do not know how to express my opinion so that people can understand it clearly. I will give you an example. It could be that the young gentleman will do something at school that will seem evil to his teacher and good to his classmates, for example.'

'What would that be?' asked Josef Blau.

'I am giving it as an example of something that would be good to some, evil to others.'

Was not Modlizki giving him a strange look, as if he were observing every movement of his muscles? Modlizki knew.

'There are general principles according to which one can distinguish good from evil. The law, religion, God.'

'The law,' said Modlizki. 'It states no one may take something that is another's. That, it seems to me, is basically it. Religion says one should love one's neighbour and that the poor shall go to heaven.'

'Is that not good, is that not a consolation?' said Josef Blau.

'It is good for the gentlemen and ladies.'

'They need it less than the others, Modlizki.'

'It may be I lack the education to understand it. That may be the reason why I am of a different opinion, if I may take the liberty. It is easy to love your neighbour, for a gentleman. The gentlemen and ladies have no occasion to steal. Therefore the prohibition does not apply to them. It is for their protection. If we love those who do evil unto us, offer the other cheek and so on, that's good for the gentlemen and ladies. All this will pass, we are told. We will go to heaven, that is our consolation. The first down here shall be the last up there, which is a consolation for the gentlemen and ladies. That, if you will allow me, is why our religion is so widespread.'

'Why it's so widespread?'

'I mean that it is against us and that is why they have it taught everywhere.'

'It's remarkable how you see it, Modlizki. You think the rich have used it to preserve their power?'

'The gentlemen and ladies. Love your enemies, it says. Thou shalt not steal, it says. Thou shalt not covet thy

103

neighbour's ass, it says. It is easier for a camel to go through the eye of a needle than for a rich man to enter into the kingdom of God, it says. I have read it. I have read that it was the faith of the slaves. The gentlemen and ladies fought against it, they could not understand it. Then they understood it, I have read, and spread it and set up its symbols among all the nations they subjected. They took everything from them, for they loved them and wanted to make it easier for them to go to heaven.'

Modlizki knew nothing but hatred. His hatred made him ingenious, but he remained limited and obstinate. He must not allow what Modlizki said to get inside him.

'Does it not come from God?' Josef Blau asked quietly.

Modlizki said nothing. He stared straight ahead.

'Does it not come from God?'

'Perhaps it comes from God,' said Modlizki.

'There is a divine force,' said Josef Blau. He had closed his eyes. 'Or everything would be unthinkable, don't you understand? Everything would be chance and madness, Modlizki.'

'From what I have read, educated people disagree among themselves about the existence of divine power. People have arisen to prove there is no God. Everything is accomplished, they say, according to simple, natural laws. The human spirit is bound to the body and dies with it, they say. It was the human spirit that invented God. Educated people have no need of God. But we still need Him, they say, and allow Him to continue to exist for our sake. For we have not been educated, we have not been properly brought up. It could be that we would fear nothing, if we did not fear God and the doctrine they preach. We might think that, without the consolation of heaven to look forward to, it is not worthwhile accepting our lot. We might start coveting the things that belong to the gentlemen and ladies, we might think revenge was ours. I do not often have the opportunity of talking to educated people. I see things the way a man without education or upbringing sees them. I would like to use this opportunity, if I may, to ask whether God exists or not.'

'I said He does,' said Josef Blau.

'Not just to set me on the right path, the path befitting a man of my station?'

'We belong to the same class, Modlizki, we grew up together.'

'I know that it does not behove me to remember that. I have forgotten it. I belong to the serving class.'

'So do I, Modlizki.'

'I can understand the desire to be respected in accordance with the class to which one belongs.'

Josef Blau avoided his eye. 'To which one belongs,' Modlizki had said, not 'to which one now belongs.' There was no mockery in his words. His voice did not rise and fall. But was that not a gleam of hatred in Modlizki's eye? Josef Blau knew he should get up and leave. Any moment it could be too late. For at any moment Modlizki's hatred of him could break out unrestrained. But from whom could he learn everything if not from Modlizki? Modlizki would get round to what Josef Blau wanted to know in his own good time. Josef Blau could feel it. He had to wait.

'God wants us to love our enemies,' Modlizki went on. 'God has given us a doctrine that is good and profitable for the gentlemen and to us he has given a consolation. I would not be so presumptuous as to deny the existence of God, but I know that He is against me. He is a gentleman who eats roast meat every day and has someone to clean His shoes, that's what I think. His doctrine is not good for us. We are the great mass and He is with the others. You cannot oppose it, in my opinion. Thou shalt not kill, thou shalt not steal.'

'Kill?'

'I said it as an example. They say goods could be distributed fairly. But they will not stay fairly distributed. And what is fair, I ask? I maintain, if you will allow me, that that is not what really matters. Not goods.'

He paused.

'Can one stop fearing God, I ask?' He fixed his eyes on Josef Blau.

105

'Don't, Modlizki, don't!'

What was he saying? What was he setting in motion? What was he provoking?

Modlizki gave a bow and fell silent.

'Why don't you go on? What is it, Modlizki? I have neither the right to stop you speaking, nor is that my intention. Oh God, you're driving me to despair,' he said in a strained voice. Modlizki remained silent.

'Go on, speak. What were you going to say? Where had you got to when I interrupted you?'

'I am well aware how boring this must be for an educated man. But one says this or that. My thoughts have not been trained so that people can understand them. I know we are excluded and I wish to remain so. We are a mass compared with the gentlemen and ladies, but as a mass we can do nothing that really matters, if you understand what I mean. We are up against them as individuals.'

'I understand you well, Modlizki.'

He faced the boys alone. They excluded him. They despised him. They employed unusual means.

'We can give rise to madness and despair.'

Modlizki could. If he went on talking like this for long he would drive Josef Blau to it. Was not every moment precious? Selma was at home, lying in bed. She might be running a temperature. The new-born child might be ill. It was a moment Karpel might choose to do something with the bill of exchange.

'We are a large, terrible, recalcitrant mass. I mean we could be. Then the rest would follow. We could give rise to madness and despair, each on our own. It is like dough, if you understand what I mean. We do not smile and we do not weep. We take no part, not in anything. We are modest but inconvenient, that is what I mean. Obedient, but fast or slow. We comply with everything, but in a way that confuses those who give the orders. They can find nothing to reprimand, but it is agonising, unnerving, yet when one looks at it, there is no reason for it to be. We are harmless and obedient, we keep on slipping through their fingers.'

'Like collar studs,' said Josef Blau. Modlizki gave him a questioning look. 'Nothing, nothing.'

'What I mean is that is how it could be. We will exclude ourselves from everything. We will not listen to music, only commands. There will be no parties held. If I am right, a great fear will arise. We will reject everything. Nothing can persuade us to stop thinking of where we come from. They cannot say anything. For the fact is, we are deaf and we obey. There is no way, I think, that leads from the gentlemen to me. They will be alone and we will be unbending and look at them, a great mass, so that they will despair. I am calm and the master is restless. I refuse to be led astray. I remain excluded from everything. It is not they who reject me, but I who reject everything. Master Karpel comes and says, "Here's a thing, Modlizki." I do not ask, I remain silent. The master and the young gentlemen do me the honour of taking me into their confidence. I only reply when I am asked a question.'

'A thing? What kind of thing? Tell me, Modlizki, tell me.'

'A thing about a bill of exchange. He had bought it, the young gentleman said.'

'What does he mean to do with it? Did he say, Modlizki?'

'The young gentleman gave no further comment.'

'No further comment? But a smile, perhaps, a smile, and his voice, did it sound pleased, mocking, what did you notice, tell me just how it happened and anything else you know, all the details, keep nothing from me, Modlizki, I beg you, we went to school . . .'

He fell silent. He felt Modlizki staring fixedly at him. Not a muscle moved in Modlizki's face as Josef Blau spoke, breathing fast, his hands raised.

'Everything could be at stake, Modlizki,' he said in a low voice, closing his eyes.

'Perhaps the young gentleman did smile. But I cannot remember. I was outside the house. It was evening. The young gentleman came along. He showed me the piece of paper. "Look," he said, "I've bought it." '

'He had it in his hand?'

'I saw it and I saw the signature. I saw that it is not yet due. When it is, it will be presented, no doubt about that.'

'No doubt? It was for Bobek, Modlizki. He's pouring it down his throat and stuffing it into his belly. I have nothing, you know, nothing. I haven't risen in the world, Modlizki, we economise and at the end of the month there's nothing left, and then all the business with the midwife, the doctor, it'll all cost money, where is it going to come from, and this on top of everything if Bobek leaves me in the lurch. You think I've got savings? Nothing, I'm as poor as the rest, as poor as you, don't you see, Modlizki? You think I've risen in the world, Modlizki? I can sense it, Modlizki, don't deny it, I can sense that you think that, but it's not true, I have nothing, Modlizki.'

'That is not the point,' said Modlizki.

'That is the point, Modlizki, the whole point, don't you see? Karpel knows that, that's why he bought the bill of exchange. He will be hard, he thinks, when the time comes and I can't pay. They have me where they want me. I have to acquiesce or they will present the bill. How did Selma come to hear about it?'

'I have no knowledge of that.'

'Who has an interest in her knowing, I ask? The person who wants me to hear about it. If I don't know, there's no point to the whole business. That's why she was told. Only Karpel can have told her.'

'It is possible the young gentleman told her.'

Josef Blau stood up and Modlizki rose at the same time. Blau quickly sat down again and waved Modlizki back to his seat.

'Does that mean he knows her, talks to her? Threatens her, frightens her, oh God, what does he demand of her? Where does he meet her, since when, you know that, he takes you into his confidence, tell me, Modlizki.'

'I have no knowledge of that.'

'Ask him, Modlizki, I must know, I need to be prepared, for everything, there's a lot brewing. There's the new teacher, Modlizki.'

'The young gentlemen talked about that.'

'About what? That he talked to Selma?'

'They spoke approvingly of him.'

'Approvingly? And what else?'

'No more was said on that subject.'

'You must ask them, Modlizki. They'll tell you. You're clever. You can worm it out of them. About the new teacher and what's happening with the bill of exchange. What should I do, Modlizki?'

'With your permission, I do not think the young gentleman will hand over the bill of exchange willingly.'

'What should I do? You must help me, Modlizki.'

Modlizki was silent. He looked at Josef Blau. Then he said, speaking slowly, 'Perhaps if you had the young gentleman in your power . . .' He hesitated. What was it? Was he checking the effect of his words?

'I don't understand. Go on.'

'Well, if the teacher had the pupil where he wanted him, as the pupil does the teacher.'

'For God's sake speak clearly. What should I do?'

'With your permission, and if you see my meaning, the young gentleman should meet his teacher in the evening. Then it is my opinion the young gentleman would be prepared to make considerable concessions. There is a lot at stake, both at home and at school'

'How do you mean, meet?'

'I mean when the young gentleman is in Kasernengasse.'

'No!' Josef Blau leapt up. 'That is impossible!'

Modlizki had risen too.

'I do not mean that the young gentleman should meet his teacher in one of those houses there. It could be that as he leaves the bawdy-house his teacher is standing outside. It will be tonight, after seven, that the young gentleman is in one of the houses. If you will allow me to say so, it will be the second house on the left, counting from the barracks. It could be his teacher is standing there as we leave the house.'

'Standing there, Modlizki . . . that is . . .'

'I could look out of the window when the time has come and give a sign that we were about to leave the house.'

'How should I . . .' He was interrupted by the shrill sound of a bell ringing.

'The master has woken,' said Modlizki.

'Yes, the bell, I heard, but we haven't finished, Modlizki.'

'With your permission, I think everything has been said. I will look out of the window in any case. It is time to make up your mind.'

'I haven't made up my mind, Modlizki. I mean, if someone should see me . . .' Modlizki was already heading for the door.

'It is part of the nature of my position that I am obliged to carry out my master's orders promptly. Delays caused by matters of a personal nature would be inappropriate. The relationship between my master and me is not a personal one. Otherwise it would not answer.'

'An exception, today, request . . .'

'I would not be understood.'

They were standing on the steps. Josef Blau's eye fell on the white, casually graceful goddess.

'It is a copy of an ancient Greek statue,' said Modlizki, 'made of Carrara marble. The master says it is a comfort to look on.'

He bowed, went back into the house and closed the door behind him. Josef Blau watched him go. How had Modlizki guessed he was thinking about the goddess? Modlizki was right, they should smash it to pieces, everything. It was there to distract them, seduce them, make them forget. Now Modlizki would be observing him through a window or a spy-hole. He found it disturbing being exposed to his eye and not seeing his face, from which the mask would have fallen away. It would be laughing, or distorted by hatred. Josef Blau went down the steps and along the gravel path through the garden. With a buzz, the gate clicked open when he reached it. He went out into the street. It was six o'clock. There was an hour left for him to make up his mind. He had to think about it calmly. What would happen when he found himself face to face with Karpel and Modlizki? If Karpel, giving everything up for lost, went for him, kicked up a fuss, drew other people? Women, drunken men would come out of the bawdy-houses, a crowd would form, Karpel would address him in a loud, mocking voice, or he would start to beg for mercy, in front of all those witnesses. How easily it might happen that Josef Blau could not flee because of the press of people round him! Modlizki could help him if he took Karpel by the arm, exploited the boy's initial surprise to drag him away. He should have requested Modlizki to do so, should have pointed out the possibility, which would not occur to Modlizki.

Josef Blau was still standing outside the house. If he rang the bell, Modlizki would have to open the door. It would only take a second for Josef Blau to whisper his request to Modlizki. His master would not notice anything. It could not be unusual for someone to ring the bell, a messenger, the postman, the woman who delivered the newspaper, a beggar.

Josef Blau pressed the bell. He waited. There was no buzz at the gate. Modlizki did not open it, did not want to talk any more. He had given his advice. He left it to Josef Blau to make up his mind. There was no way of obliging Modlizki to hear what he had to say. Josef Blau had to leave the vicinity of the house. Soon Karpel might come for Modlizki. Karpel must not meet his teacher outside Modlizki's house.

Josef Blau slowly made his way into town. It was still light. If he decided to take Modlizki's advice, he would have to turn up his coat collar and pull his hat down over his eyes. Modlizki would recognise him, he was expecting to see him there. Josef Blau would go into the street from the barracks. Then he would only have to go a few steps along Kasernengasse. The barracks was used as a public thoroughfare. He could pause for a while outside the second house, light a cigar, take out his watch, look round as if he were waiting for someone. But by that time they must come out. Kasernengasse was narrow. There was no doubt that there would be women in the entrances or in the street who would call out to him. But if he was prepared for that, then it would not cause him to turn round, as happens automatically when people are addressed unexpectedly. In that way he could halt any further approach. Once his pupil had seen him he must retrace his steps. The route through the barracks was shorter than going down to the other end of the street. He felt that once under the entrance arch of the barracks, he would be safe. Karpel would not follow him there, nor a crowd of the women. In addition Modlizki would prevent the boy from hurrying after his teacher. It was crucial that Josef Blau should not stay a fraction of a second longer than was necessary once Karpel had seen him. It could all be over in a few minutes, as long as nothing unforeseen occurred. There was no need for anything to be said. Now there was something Josef Blau could use against his pupil, if he followed Modlizki's advice.

He went into a cigar shop and bought a cigar and a box of matches. He could make all the preparations without having taken the final decision. It could be that would come so late there would be no time left to procure the cigar and matches. The cigar was important. A man stopping in the street, taking out a cigar, meticulously cutting off the end, taking out his matches and lighting his cigar was an everyday sight no one would give a second glance. Moreover in that way the wait would be broken up into activity, would be occupied and more bearable. He would know what he had to concentrate on while he was waiting – the cigar, the flickering match – until the door opened.

It was half past six by the time he reached the city centre. Walking slowly, it was no more than five minutes from there to Kasernengasse. The street lamps came on in the main street. But it was still day, though perhaps softened by the onset of twilight. The opportunity of catching Karpel out might not come again so soon. There could be no objection to Modlizki's proposal. Karpel was resorting to unusual means, his teacher would respond in an unusual way. No one, not even Karpel, would assume he had gone to Kasernengasse for any other reason than to catch Karpel. Otherwise he would not be standing waiting outside the house Karpel came out of. It must be clear that Karpel's activities had been reported to his teacher and that the teacher had now come to this place to catch Karpel in the act. If the street was too busy he would be able to see that from the safety of the barracks entrance. He would abandon the enterprise and turn back. Perhaps the street was quiet at this time of day. Anyone coming towards him could be recognised, from a distance. As long as he was in the barracks, he was secure. He could go in without having made up his mind and have a quick look to see what things were like in the street.

There were guards and groups of soldiers standing in the gateway. He crossed the wide parade-ground. Soldiers were drawn up in lines. An officer was reading out a document in a loud voice. Josef Blau went through a second gate into a dark hallway. He turned up his coat collar and pulled his hat down over his eyes. There was a guard standing at the exit from the hallway. Josef Blau hesitated for a moment. Kasernengasse stretched out before him. A single soldier with a briefcase under his arm was coming along the street towards the gate.

The cigar and the box of matches were in Josef Blau's pocket. His heart was pounding, his breath coming in short gasps. The soldier beside him was looking at him. The soldier with the briefcase came in. He shouted something to the guard and walked past Josef Blau. Steps on the stone flags could be heard approaching out of the darkness of the hallway behind Josef Blau. The street in front of Josef Blau was empty. He went out into it, walking slowly, like someone out for a stroll. Shapes in the darkness of the doorways resolved themselves into hatless women in loose, sleeveless dresses and shawls round their shoulders. Josef Blau had not noticed them from the barracks gate. Behind the window-panes he saw round, flat faces, pale in the glimmer of the street-lights, with big round eyes. To his right someone tapped on the window with their knuckles. He did not look round. A window clattered open. The women in the doorways beckoned him over with their heads and called out to him in soft, lisping voices. Someone was coming up behind him, presumably in slippers. He could hear their steps shuffling over the cobbles. A woman's voice called out after him. His hand clutched the cigar in his pocket tight. Now he was outside the second house on the left.

Could he stop? All around were beckoning heads and hands and soft, lisping voices. Before him was the longer portion of the street, another hundred yards to the end. He must return to the safety of the barracks! Had Modlizki seen him? Josef Blau had turned up his coat collar and pulled his hat down over his eyes. He decided to turn back.

The door of the second house was opened from the inside. A beam of light fell on the cobbles in front of Josef Blau. Someone went past a female figure and out into the street. It was not Karpel. Behind him, still in the hallway, Josef Blau saw two figures. He recognised Modlizki by the way he held his head. Was that Karpel standing beside him? This was the decisive moment. Josef Blau straightened up. A cry rang out. The door slammed shut. It was Laub, the pupil in his class, who had cried out. He was standing in the street, alone. Now Josef Blau recognised him. The others were in the house. Laub raised his hands, his hat had fallen off. He had very fair hair with a parting. He was going towards his teacher.

There was no time to lose. A crowd might gather. The women would side with the pupil. Josef Blau turned round. He ran back up the street to the barracks. The schoolboy followed him. He heard his voice. It called out something but Josef Blau could not understand what it said. He ran through the barracks. He stopped in a wide street with trees along it. He leant against a tree. His heart was pounding.

'The other was Karpel,' he thought. 'He's in my power.'

He looked round. Laub was no longer following him. Josef Blau took a deep breath and straightened up. He threw his arms wide and stretched, as if a burden had fallen off his back. He smiled. He could await further developments with equanimity. He was a resourceful planner and he executed his plans with vigour. He could go home reassured.

At home he found Selma's mother and Bobek in the living-room. Selma had been sleeping. He glanced in at her and Josef Albert. Selma nodded to him.

He still had his coat on. As he started to take it off he realised he still had the cigar in his left hand. He placed it on the table in front of Uncle Bobek.

'There,' he said, 'have a smoke.'

He smiled. He could have patted Bobek on the shoulder, he thought, and said, 'Old boy.'

Chapter Ten

Uncle Bobek lit the cigar after dinner. Leaning back, eyes half closed, he took his first puffs.

Uncle Bobek was still blissfully unaware. Now it was to be his turn. Josef Blau intended to continue as he had begun, to clear everything out of the way, to put things in order. He had not finished yet. The money must be found, without delay, it had to be paid and Uncle Bobek must find it. The bill of exchange had to disappear, even if Karpel would not risk anything now. The bill of exchange threatened them, it remained a danger as long as the money was not there, and there was no other way of getting it.

Uncle Bobek watched the smoke he was blowing out. He was dreaming. Josef Blau was going to say just a few words, clear, calm words that brooked no argument, that Uncle Bobek would not be able to ignore. Then he would go to Selma and tell her that everything was in order. Selma must look up to him; he was bold and resolute. Karpel would not risk anything now. Josef Blau protected Selma, he foiled plots which threatened Selma and the baby, she was safe with Josef Blau, even if he was no gymnast like the new teacher.

Uncle Bobek did not feel Josef Blau's eye on him. He saw nothing, he was smoking. Uncle Bobek was happy. But was Josef Blau not also happy? Had Josef Blau's happiness not also begun now? Uncle Bobek's happiness was about to be clouded for a moment. But Selma's mother would pour him some wine, she would set some rich, spicy food before him and the clouds would dissipate. Uncle Bobek was not a man to grieve.

'You'll join me in a glass of wine?' said Josef Blau.

Uncle Bobek opened his eyes.

'Yes, yes.' Josef Blau smiled at him. Why should he not have a drink with Bobek? 'There must be some left.'

'Blau,' said Uncle Bobek, 'you're a man after my own heart.'

Josef Blau leant back. He was the first of the two to raise his glass and hold it up to the light. Glass raised, he toasted fat Bobek.

Uncle Bobek looked at him in disbelief. He too raised his glass.

'Blau,' he repeated, 'you're a man after my own heart.'

Did Bobek like him? Well, perhaps everyone would like him now. Selma, the class, the new teacher. Everything was easy once you knew how to go about it.

Josef Blau did not lean forward when he told Bobek. He looked up at the ceiling. He said calmly that the money had to be there by the next day and that one of his pupils had bought the bill of exchange. Uncle Bobek stared down at the table-top.

'Well? Josef Blau asked.

Uncle Bobek did not fly into a rage, he kept his head bowed. He submitted to Josef Blau as if there were no alternative but to submit to Josef Blau.

'Mathilda, my dear,' said Uncle Bobek, 'you heard him. The money has to be there by tomorrow. Will you advance it, Mathilda dear?'

'Under certain circumstances,' Selma's mother shouted.

Bobek was breathing heavily. On the table in front of him lay the bare, fleshy arm of Selma's mother. Slowly he stretched out his hand. He gave Josef Blau a questioning look. But Josef Blau did not smile. His eyes were fixed mercilessly on Bobek.

Hesitantly Uncle Bobek placed his hand on Selma's mother's arm. Then he bowed his head. 'Those circumstances have come into effect, Mathilda dear,' he said quietly.

Selma's mother stood up.

'That means . . .?'

Uncle Bobek nodded.

'Bobek!' Selma's mother went over to Uncle Bobek. She embraced him and kissed him on the lips.

'It's all right,' said Uncle Bobek. 'You pay the money.'

Selma's mother grasped him and pulled him over to Josef Blau. She embraced Josef Blau, without letting go of Bobek.

Blau felt her wet lips on his cheek. Uncle Bobek was chewing his cigar.

'Oh,' Selma's mother shouted, 'oh, Bobek!' She leant her head on his chest.

Uncle Bobek took a step backwards. 'We must control our urges, Mathilda,' he said. They went to see Selma in her bed. Her mother snuggled up against Bobek's shoulder.

'Oh Selma, Selma,' she sobbed. 'Just you look at us. It's happened. Yes, yes, I'm going to have to leave you.'

Selma smiled. She held out her hand and took her mother's, who bent over Selma and kissed her, sobbing all the time.

'No, no,' said Selma's mother, 'this . . . if anyone had told me yesterday . . . You give her a kiss too, Bobek.' She dried her tears with a crumpled handkerchief. 'Tell her you'll be a good father to her, Bobek, oh, oh, he's been dead for eighteen years now, eighteen years, how time passes, he wasn't to be here to see it. No one would ever have thought it would be Bobek. Why don't you say something, Bobek.'

'Words fail me,' said Uncle Bobek. 'It's no small matter, God knows. After all, I was my own master. The way I'm used to things, I don't like talking in the morning, only after I've got something warm inside me, you understand, not before. I would have thought there's still time. You won't want to rush into things, Mathilda, perhaps we should think it over again.'

'Everything has been thought over,' said Josef Blau.

'Fine, fine. Just a thought. A suggestion, that's all. No offence, my dears. It's just that it's all happened so quickly. You have to get used to the idea.'

He went out of the room with Selma's mother clinging to his arm.

'Now everything will be sorted out,' said Josef Blau. 'Your mother's going to give Uncle Bobek the money now.'

He was standing by Selma's bed.

'I'm so happy,' said Selma. She smiled and nodded at him.

Karpel would give back the bill of exchange if Josef Blau had the money, and he would have it in the morning. That would be that sorted out. But that was not everything. At bottom it was not important. When you thought about it, what could Karpel have done with the bill of exchange? It was not because of the bill of exchange alone that Josef Blau had gone to Kasernengasse. The other thing was more important, the fact that she could only have heard about it from Karpel. Now he could ask her. She could not escape him. She would speak. He had succeeded in everything so far, he would succeed in this too. He would know whether she met Karpel, where and how often she had seen him and everything that had happened.

'Who told you about it, Selma?'

She was no longer smiling.

'About the bill of exchange,' he said.

She avoided his eye.

'I'm not to say,' she said in a low voice.

'Tell me. You must speak, Selma.'

She remained silent.

'Why are you asking me?' she said.

'I have to know,' was what he was about to say. But he did not say it. What was the real reason he was asking her? Whatever it was, whether Karpel had told her or someone else, it was past. Now Selma would see Josef Blau as he really was, clever and resourceful, resolute and full of greatness of soul. Why did he need to know?

He forgave. He forgot. Now that all lay far behind them. He smiled. They looked at each other. And now she was laughing, they were both laughing, for no reason, out loud, not so loud that Uncle Bobek and Selma's mother in the other room could hear it, but loud enough to wake Josef Albert.

'Good night, Selma,' said Josef Blau.

'Good night.'

He was still smiling as he came into the living-room.

Uncle Bobek had taken off his jacket. On the table were three full glasses.

Selma's mother was speaking in a loud voice. Uncle Bobek was staring into space and drinking.

'My room will be empty now,' she said to Josef Blau. 'But perhaps you'll let it out.' She wiped the tears from her cheeks.

Sobbing, she went over to the picture of her first husband that was hanging on the wall.

'Will you be as good a husband to me as he was, Bobek?' She pointed at the picture. Uncle Bobek did not reply. 'He loved me, he was very affectionate towards me. Why should I be ashamed to admit it?'

She took the picture off the wall, breathed on the glass and rubbed at it with her handkerchief.

'Kosterhoun, Kosterhoun,' she cried, 'you can have had no idea, Kosterhoun, that your Hilduschka and fat Bobek . . . no idea . . .'

She went to the table and leant over Uncle Bobek. 'Will you call me Hilduschka as well, Bobek?'

Uncle Bobek looked up and slapped his hand on the table. 'No,' he said, 'not that. You won't get me to do that Mathilda. All right, all right, I'm not saying no. It's not due yet, but I'll do it. When does Bobek think of himself? But you must put the idea I'll call you that right out of your mind, as sure as my name's Bobek. If you think I'm going to let people ride rough-shod over me you've all got another think coming.'

He emptied his glass, poured himself another, drank that one and slammed the glass down on the table.

We ought to be celebrating, thought Josef Blau, differently, with music, singing, Herr Leopold ought to be here, there ought to be speeches, he himself, Josef Blau, wanted to speak. Selma would hear him and compare. He wanted to drink and to dance with Selma. He raised his glass to Uncle Bobek.

'Did you hear that, Blau?' Uncle Bobek said. 'Hilduschka! Did you hear? I'm an easy-going fellow, but everything has its limits. It might be possible to get rid of it in another way, but all right, all right. I've said yes and I'll do it. And why? Have you thought about that?' The tears welled up. 'I'm doing it for you, that's the way I am, that's the way I've always been. But we must have a celebration, d'you hear? Something people will talk about, the way Uncle Bobek celebrated his engagement. There's no getting out of it, Mathilda, no excuses. And stick your Kosterhoun back on the wall, goddammit!'

'He's so covered in dust, poor Kosterhoun,' said Selma's mother and hung the picture back on its hook.

Uncle Bobek emptied his glass.

'I can't get in the mood,' he said. 'All because of that bit of money. You know, Blau, that's the way it is. You walk blindly into things, who thinks where they will end? Yes, yes, if you only knew how things were going to turn out, but you can't, all you can do is trust in God, and what does that change? How often do you find it's not been worthwhile and you can't go back, you know, you want to tear your hair out, but what's the use? Why worry your head, I always say. Every cloud has a silver lining. I'm not as young as I was and now I've got someone to tuck me in, make up the hot-water bottle and warm my nightshirt at the stove and see that there's always something good to eat and some schnapps to drink in the house. Every cloud has a silver lining. But what's that? Can you hear it? Who do they want? Perhaps it's some friends, go and let them in, Blau, I need them, tell them to come up, I want to see them, face to face, they must cheer me up and have a drink with us.'

Josef Blau could hear it too. Someone was clapping their hands down in the street. Then the clapping stopped, to be replaced by whistles and shouts.

Josef Blau drew back the curtain and opened the window. He saw two figures in the dark street.

'Hello there,' one of them called out.

It was Modlizki's voice.

What did Modlizki want from him? And who was the other person standing beside Modlizki. He couldn't see. Perhaps it was Laub or Karpel. They must have come because he had seen them. They were going to beg him for forgiveness, that must be it. Let them come. It was all so far in the past now. He bore no malice. He forgave.

'Throw the key down to him,' said Uncle Bobek.

Selma's mother wrapped the key to the front door in a sheet of newspaper. Then she threw it out of the window.

Modlizki came in by himself. So the other one must still be down there. He was afraid to come up.

'Take a seat,' said Uncle Bobek. 'Come and join in our family celebration. Aren't you part of it, really? You're Blau's friend, that's enough.'

'I would not refuse your invitation, Herr Bobek,' said Modlizki, 'but it's a serious matter I've come about.'

'You want to be alone. Fine, I understand. Friends sometimes have things to say to each other. We'll go to your room Mathilda. Call us when you've finished. I'm having a quiet day today, we must keep each other company. I don't want to be alone, you see.'

Modlizki closed the door carefully behind them. 'I beg you to forgive me, but I felt it was important to tell you what has happened as soon as I heard about it.'

'What is it, Modlizki? I saw everything, Modlizki. Karpel was with you in the hall. He closed the door, but it was too late. I recognised him.'

'It is not the young gentleman I have come about. He is waiting for me outside.'

'He could have come up with you, Modlizki. I'm not angry with him. You will get the money and Karpel will hand over the bill of exchange. That is all I want, nothing more.'

'That is not what I have come about.'

'Not what you have come about?'

'The young gentleman does not want anything.'

'I saw Karpel, Modlizki. But that is sufficient, you see. You don't have to speak up for him, if that is what he is asking you to do.'

'It is the other young gentleman I have come about.'

'Laub? Is he there too? Tell them I know they will remember this evening. You can go home now, Modlizki.'

'The other young gentleman is not there. We caught up with him outside the barracks. The young gentleman was very upset. We took him along some quiet streets. The young gentleman was sobbing and nothing we said was able to calm him down. The young gentleman has been very strictly brought up. It was well after eight o'clock before he had calmed down. "Forgive me," he said then, "it's just my nerves. I got a terrible fright. Theresa made such a horrible face, with his mouth open wide." He was referring to his teacher. Then he started to laugh. We thought he had got over it. When we were alone . . .'

Modlizki paused.

'We thought it was the plan we had made that had calmed him down. I was to go and beg leniency for him in the morning. Only we could not get his final laugh out of our minds. There was something eerie about it I can't describe. We walked around together for another hour, but we did not speak about it. We were drawn to the house where the young gentleman lives. I'm always surprised at how differently the young gentlemen see things, but I hadn't reckoned with that.'

'With what?'

'That the young gentleman would hang himself.'

Josef Blau drew back. His hands felt for something to hold on to.

'Modlizki!' he screamed.

'It happened and it surprised us all.'

Josef Blau went up to him. He grasped him by the shoulder.

'You're lying,' he wanted to shout. But his throat had lost the power over his voice.

Blau's hand slipped off Modlizki's shoulder.

'We decided to come here. It seemed a sensible precaution to let his teacher know.'

'And Laub, Modlizki?' Josef Blau's voice was hoarse. His mouth was dry.

'It appears he did it as soon as he got home. He was seen from the street. The light was on in the room and the young gentleman was hanging from the cross-piece of the window. They had already cut him down when we arrived.'

'He's . . .?'

'The young gentleman must have been hanging there for an hour. It is impossible for anyone to survive that. It is beyond the power of a human being. He had changed as far as the colour of his face was concerned. The young gentleman's tongue . . .'

'Oh God, Modlizki, oh God!'

He collapsed into the chair and put his head in his hands on the table. He heard a thin, tearful voice from the next room. When was it that the sun had fallen on Laub's bare head? His hair had shone as if it were made of silver. The boy's face was as delicate as a girl's, red and white, still with downy cheeks. Modlizki was speaking, his voice did not rise and fall. But perhaps Josef Blau was dreaming. That must be it, he was dreaming. Had he not changed? What was it Modlizki was talking about? Josef Blau could not understand, it went straight past him.

'There will be an investigation. They will ask how it came about. They know the young gentleman was out with young Master Karpel. They will ask where they had been. Master Karpel is going to say that they were in the park. Master Laub was in a playful mood, he will say. They will expect there to have been something striking about the young gentleman's behaviour. Master Karpel is going to say that it struck him that the young gentleman was more playful than usual. That is what I have advised him. It is essential to discuss it straight away.'

Josef Blau was silent.

'Young Master Karpel is waiting for me. It is essential the young gentleman be told what he is to say. If no one says what actually happened, then the young gentleman can say what I have advised him to say. Otherwise the young gentleman will have to tell them that Master Laub cried out as he left the bawdy-house and that he was in despair.'

Modlizki waited.

'So what shall it be when the time comes? The parents will come looking for someone to blame. For that is a consolation in grief.'

Josef Blau lifted up his head.

'And who is to blame? Who caused it, they will say when they hear that, who is to blame for his death? His teacher, Herr Professor Blau murdered him.'

Josef Blau stood up. He looked at Modlizki with a fixed, unmoving stare. Modlizki drew back. Josef Blau's hands were feeling round on the table, as if they were searching for something. They took hold of the wine bottle. The fingers clutched the neck as if they were trying to choke it. Modlizki ducked. Josef Blau had raised the wine bottle. He swung it up over his head. The wine ran down his sleeve. Josef Blau's mouth was open. He emitted a hoarse sound. Then the bottle smashed against the wall.

Josef Blau leant on the table. He was holding one hand to his mouth. Something warm and sticky was dribbling out of his mouth and over his fingers. Was it blood? Laub's blood that was on his hands? He raised his hands, he was spinning round and round, then more blood came, he had to stuff his hands into his mouth, to block the hole, Bobek, Selma's mother, Modlizki were going round and round him. Now they were tugging at him. He did not resist. He closed his eyes.

Selma's mother brought some water. Modlizki offered to fetch the doctor.

'A haemorrhage,' Modlizki said. 'One of his pupils hanged himself because he was seen in a bawdy-house. Herr Blau has taken it too much to heart.'

'Hold me tight, Bobek,' said Selma's mother.

'Isn't that what I said, Mathilda? He's not well, Mathilda. Germs the size of dates, that's how I usually put it. Open the window, Mathilda.'

He turned to Modlizki. 'The youth of today have no religion, Herr Modlizki. They don't put their faith in God the way we used to. Didn't I go to the bawdy-house when I was fifteen? But did I kill myself? I ask you, Herr Modlizki, did I do that?'

'You did not, Herr Bobek,' Modlizki replied. He bowed and left the room.

Chapter Eleven

Everything was clear, a closed circle. Nowhere was there a gap. Everything was fulfilled. Josef Blau had a fever. During the nights his body was damp with cold sweat. Josef Blau kept his eyes closed. But his head was clear.

The dark dreams of the first days had gone. He was no longer running away, heart pounding, with heavy lumps of thick mud on his feet. He no longer saw, as if drawn on a pale sheet of paper, the face of his pupil, Laub, with his swollen tongue clamped between his teeth, and behind him Modlizki, surrounded by the boys from the class, dressed in black, waxen faced, in his hand a curving top hat from which a band of crepe fluttered in an inexplicable breeze. For there was not a breath of air, everything was absolutely still, motionless.

Now there was a cool clarity in Josef Blau's brain. Like a summer's morning after a sultry night, he thought. Josef Blau did not want to see, nor to speak. He did not want the clarity to go away. Everything was clear. He understood everything. He did not cry and he did not pray. It was too late for crying, or speaking, or praying. It was too late to call on God, to wring his hands, to think up words of entreaty. Laub, his pupil, was dead. It was not some inexorable fate that had brought death to him, Laub's death had a beginning somewhere, at some point the path to Laub's death branched off, it started at some point, at some point came the step off the path of life onto the path of death. It was impossible to go back to that point, to start afresh.

Where had it begun? Had it begun with the cigar Josef Blau had bought? Without the cigar Josef Blau would not have gone to Kasernengasse and Laub would still be alive. But that was not the beginning. Had it started with his conversation with Modlizki, with the words Selma had whispered to Josef Blau as he stood by her bed after the birth of Josef Albert, with the bill of exchange, with Uncle Bobek, with Josef Albert?

Wherever it had begun, it was irreversible, every word, every step had made a difference to the path. Every word, every step had consequences, every time anyone acted, they burdened themselves with guilt, entangled themselves and others. The path went to and fro, from one to the other, from Josef Blau to Selma, to Karpel, to Selma's mother, to Bobek, to Josef Albert, to Herr Leopold, to Laub. They were all caught up in it, they were all interconnected. Everything you said or did continued, you could not see which way it went or where it ended. You could not go back to the beginning, could not start afresh, and there was no end to it. Josef Blau had acted, had made plans and carried them through. Laub was in his grave, and in his cot lay Josef Albert, the heir to all the entanglement, all the sin, all the suffering. Josef Blau understood his own guilt: he had acted, knowing that every act contains within it the force of further acts, he had breathed, knowing that the only way to remain free from guilt was to be like a tree, not breathing, inert, not thinking, for what had been thought was also part of the world. Everyone sensed that was the way it was, but only those who had been overcome by God saw it through to the end, and for them there was no way out. Oh, every breath changed the world. If only you could hold your breath and thus remain guiltless. It started with your first word, your first cry. Perhaps his pupil had already been dying before he was born, when Josef Blau, the instrument of his death, not a blameless instrument, was born, took his first breath, gave his first cry, took his first step, went out holding his mother's hand. His mother was carrying Josef Blau's brother wrapped up in her arms. She covered up his face so that no eye could see it, for it might be an evil eye that fixed on him. The women came up to his mother and asked how old the baby was. His mother sensed what a word could do, a word of praise, presumptuous, tempting fate, it was capable of calling the child's happiness, the child's life into question, and she tried to protect the baby, saying it was a year old when it was only six months. Had Laub's death begun with the death of that boy, who had died in infancy? With the tears and prayers of its mother, who quickly followed it? She had hollow cheeks, she did the washing for her husband and son in the kitchen, she lifted heavy weights and she railed against God until the blood came out of her throat and she had to die. Everything continued and carried on and now the blood had come out of Josef Blau's mouth and where would it end? One thing rested on another and one followed on another. You could go back, step by step, but you could not bring anything back to life. Had it started with his father, the ex-soldier, the court usher who groaned as he tossed and turned in his bed at night so that the boards creaked, who had brought him into the world as Josef Blau, irrevocably, just as Josef Blau had Josef Albert? One boy was called Kurt Wünsche and was the son of the judge, and one was Josef Blau, wore a waistcoat, assisted the priest at the altar in a white surplice together with Modlizki, became a teacher, because one thing follows on another, words and steps without number, because this man had fathered him, was his father and was the way he was, and this woman his mother, that the room where he was born, that the name he had been given, this the night when he lay awake, and this the other when he slept, because he had encountered one thing and avoided another, an endless chain. He stood in front of the class and acted and spoke, and Laub, his pupil, was dead and other things were already set, already in motion, unstoppable, and no one even suspected. He stood in front of them and spoke and moved and countered their plans with his plans. He commanded them and merely standing in front of them in silence had marked them indelibly, whether it aroused love, or hatred, or indifference. Other men were farmers, merchants or officials, they were not so much caught up, the fate of many others, were not responsible to divine justice for them, as Josef Blau was. They did not realise, as Josef Blau realised, for his mind was all clarity now, that there was no escape, no way out, nowhere to flee to, that you could not escape, that there was nothing that did not have consequences. It was no use keeping your eyes closed, it was impossible to shut down everything apart from breathing, you should not think, but the thoughts went through your brain, one following the other. Perhaps he should try counting, as he had done as a child when sleep would not come, do nothing but count until everything was over.

Someone was bending over him. He opened his eyes. It was broad daylight. Selma was standing by his bedside. How many days was it since Modlizki had brought the news of Laub's death? Then Selma had still been in bed with a fever. Now she was once more as beautiful as she had been before she bore Josef Albert. There were no lines round her eyes now and her cheeks were red. She had opened her mouth, half raised her hands. What had frightened her? Where was Josef Albert? He could not hear him. Was he asleep or was he dead? But he must not think, he must count, nothing but count, he was already counting, he was counting out loud, that was why Selma had come to his bedside. He gestured with his head for her to come closer. She bent over him.

'Paper,' he whispered.

She brought a sheet of paper and a pencil. He put the paper on his knee. He wrote numbers on the paper, four-figure numbers. He added them up and subtracted them from each other. She placed her hand on his arm.

'What's that?' she said. 'Oh God, what's happened?'

She was crying.

He could hear her. But how could he explain it to her? Who could understand who had not been overcome by it?

She removed her hand. She did not take her eyes off him until, bent exhausted over the sheet of paper, he fell asleep.

When he awoke, Modlizki was standing at the foot of his bed. It must have been about four o'clock in the afternoon. Modlizki had his head tilted to one side. His voice was as monotonous as that of the precentor in church. Where was his top hat? Perhaps he was holding it in such a way that the bedstead concealed it.

'It is all over,' said Modlizki, 'and there is no cause for concern. That is why I have come. Everything happened as planned. The interment of the young gentleman's mortal remains was carried out with due solemnity. The funeral rites were attended by the young gentleman's sorely tried father, his grief-stricken mother, the entire teaching staff in mourning and young gentlemen from all the classes. With a tasteful selection of music, in keeping with the young gentleman's station in society, the ceremony was a complete success. I joined in the funeral procession myself. Young Master Karpel was deeply moved. I accompanied him home to comfort him.'

It is an apparition, thought Josef Blau. It is out of a dream.

'As I said, there is no cause for concern. The investigation was carried out in a superficial manner. Should I give you a report on it?'

'No thank you,' said Josef Blau.

He picked up the sheet of paper that was beside the bed and bent over it. He started multiplying six-figure numbers.

When Josef Blau looked up again, Martha was sitting at his bedside. There was no one else in the room. When Josef Blau turned to face Martha, she started. She was sitting, bolt upright, on the edge of the chair, ready to jump up and shout for help.

Later in the afternoon the new teacher, Herr Leopold, came in. He sat down by the head of the bed. Selma had come in at the same time. She must have opened the door for him. She sat down on the opposite side to Herr Leopold, at the foot of the bed. He was wearing a blue suit with the corner of a white silk handkerchief hanging out of his left breast pocket.

'I'm glad to see you're awake again,' said Herr Leopold. Since he had seen him in a different state, that meant he must have been there during Blau's illness, often, perhaps every day. 'And you're occupying yourself, that's a good sign. Is it a specific problem you're working on, Herr Blau?'

'Multiplications,' Josef Blau replied, 'multiplications with six-figure numbers.'

'Oh, I see,' said Herr Leopold earnestly.

They will think I'm mad because they don't understand, thought Josef Blau.

'It takes my mind off things,' he said, 'I don't have to think. I imagine it helps me relax. I mean it's not important in itself.'

Selma had her hands in her lap. Her fingers were crumpling a little handkerchief. Herr Leopold looked at her. There was no one to stand in their way. Josef Blau could not do that any more. He just wanted to do calculations, that had no consequences, no one would die because of it. Why had he tried to excuse it? Let them think he was mad. What difference did it make? He had seen the truth. Had not those who saw the truth first often been thought mad?

'I bring greetings from your pupils, Herr Blau,' said Herr Leopold. 'I have taken over your class until you recover. The boys' thoughts are with you during your illness. Karpel wanted to come and see you, but I did not allow it. Every day he asks me how you are. He is very attached to his teacher. Would you have liked him to come and see you?'

'No,' said Josef Blau.

'It is good to see how devoted to you your pupils are. That is the reward for the heavy responsibilities of our profession. It is a fine profession, Frau Blau. I chose it because I love it. My father, who was a senior civil servant, wanted me to become a lawyer. I have never regretted becoming a school-teacher. When you know how to deal with them, the pupils are like putty in their teacher's hands. You try to shape them, to turn them into the ideal you have in your mind. You must have a clear-cut vision of your ideal, otherwise you can make mistakes, mistakes that can never be rectified. The material the teacher works with is more precious than the most precious marble. Of course, we don't all have the same ideal of the complete man. My ideal is related to that of the ancient Greeks. Your ideal may be different, Herr Blau. It doesn't matter which ideal one is striving for, the important thing is to strive for it.'

What was he saying? Did he know what he was taking on himself? Did he have no idea of the responsibility one bore? That things turned out differently from what one intended? His voice spread over everything, it sounded pleasant and alluring, like a layer of thin ice in autumn covering the lake whose waters heaved beneath the frozen surface. It was time he left. Josef Blau did not want to hear what else Herr Leopold had to say. He closed his eyes.

'You're tired. You'll find you get better quickly once you're back in school,' said Herr Leopold. 'Exercise, activity will soon set you to rights. We'll make sure you look after yourself, Herr Blau. It's magnificent summer weather at the moment. As soon as the doctor allows, we'll take you out into the fresh air. It works wonders.'

Selma shook her head.

'Believe me, Frau Blau. The air in a stuffy room makes everything worse than it is. Everything is easier than it seems. That is part of my philosophy. Not a particularly profound belief, but healthy. I'll leave now and come back tomorrow, Herr Blau needs his rest. You come with me, Frau Selma. An hour in the sun and you'll see things really are easier.'

It was time he left, Josef Blau thought. With her or alone, as long as he doesn't stay here talking.

Selma had taken hold of Blau's hand. He opened his eyes.

'I'm staying,' she said.

Herr Leopold was standing beside her, as if he were wondering whether to go alone or not.

'If he needs me,' said Selma.

'Your presence is not required. Herr Blau will occupy himself with his multiplications. Time will pass quickly for him.'

Josef Blau looked at Herr Leopold. 'I'm not mad,' he said.

Selma gave a cry. 'What are you saying!' she exclaimed. 'Don't you know it's a sin to say things like that?'

She threw herself over Josef Blau and clasped him tight. Herr Leopold put his hand on her shoulder. Then he carefully took hold of her and lifted her up. It was obvious how strong he was. Selma's mother had come in. She put Selma's coat over her shoulders and placed her hat on her head. Herr Leopold led Selma slowly out of the room.

Selma's mother sat down in the seat Herr Leopold had been sitting in by the head of the bed. Her breathing was loud and deep. Her head sank back. Her eyes were half closed. There was a smile playing round her open lips. Why was she smiling? Was she dreaming of her own happiness, of her hope for the belated affection she would get from fat Bobek? Or was she dreaming of her daughter who, at that moment, was walking along the streets with the new teacher, who was strong and sunburnt? Was it her daughter's happiness that

131

was making her smile? The two of them belonged together, Selma and the new teacher. Everyone wanted it, her mother fetched her hat and coat, everyone knew and they smiled because what they had known from the start was coming true. No one opposed it. No one stood in their way.

Now Selma's mother had shut her eyes. She was asleep. How long had they been out? Perhaps they were sitting on a bench in the park. When it grew dark there were always men and women sitting on the benches, close together. You could hear them whispering, suddenly a match would flare up, then go out again immediately, and the glowing dots of cigarettes, now more, now less intense, would describe circles in the dark. Herr Leopold had his arm round Selma's shoulders, they were silent, Selma was leaning against his breast, she was crying, but not with sorrow any more, with joy and happiness. Perhaps they were at the cinema, holding hands. Images passed in front of them on the screen, handsome men and beautiful women who were in love, overcame all obstacles and fell into each others' arms, as had been ordained. Josef Blau was not standing in their way any more. Josef Blau must not think any thoughts, not think when she left, not think while she was out, not think when she came back. Everything had to be erased from his mind, he must not trigger off anything else in addition to what he had already triggered off and brought down on himself, on her, on the child and on another, oh, on another, on Laub, his pupil. Would his place be occupied by a different boy? Who would sit at that place? But they had left the place free, it was empty, it was a hole, a gap in the coherence of the class, they did not close the gap, it was like mocking laughter in an open mouth, they wanted him to tell them that the gap should be closed. Perhaps Karpel had suggested it, the others had agreed, they were forcing him to say it, to order it, for the place must not remain empty.

'Vacha, go and sit in Laub's place.'

His lips refused to pronounce it, he could not say it, he could not confess it. He was innocent, he had not brought death to Laub. Modlizki had desired Laub's death, he was driving them to their deaths, they were all in danger, Karpel as much as the rest, they could not escape, they must be freed. Modlizki was to blame, Modlizki had been pursuing Josef Blau, never letting up, ever since they were boys. Why did Modlizki refuse to forgive him? He could not tear himself away from Modlizki, Modlizki had sent him to Kasernengasse, Modlizki had known how it would end, it was him Josef Blau should have killed, if he was to do anything else, that must be it, he must get up, must go and free himself from Modlizki, that would be the last thing, then it would all be over, for there was nothing more for him since he understood everything now that his mind was all clarity. He could not stand in front of the pupils like Herr Leopold, for he knew now that everything had consequences and you did not know where they were going to lead. He had to disappear from view. They thought he was mad, he had seen the look on Herr Leopold's face. Perhaps it would be good to sit in a cell and be insane. Or to sit in a cell and pray. To obey the three evangelical injunctions the holy Church has given us: to live in voluntary poverty, complete chastity and absolute submission to a spiritual superior. Yes, it all began with money and carnal desire. A person who understood that could live free of guilt. He could sit there and obey, like a boy in school, not having to bear the responsibility of the teacher, nor suffer the condemnation of the judge. He would not entangle anyone else for he was not involved with anyone else but the Lord. But Josef Blau was already involved with many others. There was Josef Albert in his mother's room. For Josef Blau it was too late to follow the injunctions. What did that leave, then, for the man who had recognised that everything one did burdened one with responsibility, with guilt, that every word, every thought had consequences which could not be halted, could destroy and kill? For the man who had seen that, was there any alternative left other than the end, death? Was it even possible to recognise that, without dying from the knowledge? After having recognised that, you could not go on living, and perhaps only someone who already had death in his heart could recognise it. Was it really the clarity of a cool morning illuminating Josef Blau's mind? Was it not the clarity of a different, icy coolness, the clarity of the hour before death? Oh, he was dying, Josef Blau was dying. That was why Selma had been crying. She had understood before he had understood. But she must not cry. It was good that way, it was all over.

It was dark. Josef Blau had leant back and closed his eyes.

'Come, my Saviour,' he whispered.

Selma's mother was asleep. But Josef Albert in the next room had started to cry softly. Oh, he could sense that his father was dying. He should be happy! Nothing more would have its origin in his father, nothing more proceed from him, it was all over.

Josef Blau sat up in bed. Was it all over? It was all over for him, but was it all over around him? Would not everything he had set in motion carry on, unstoppable, unending, even if he were dead? He ceased to be, but there was no end to it! It must end for those around him, everything, what he had passed on, what he had triggered off, must not continue, oh God, oh God, he must not continue to sweep others along with him, not his son, lying guiltless in his cot, not the boys at school, not Selma, it had to stop, halt, break off, not continue, dry up like a stream in the desert. He had to have a sign that nothing that came from him would live on when he was dead. Even if he had never succeeded before, now he must reach the place where things were decided, he wanted a sign that he had been heard, a sign before he died, for he had to die, a sign that it was all over for those around him, a sign, a sign!

He got out of bed. Selma's mother was asleep. He felt his way to the bedroom door. He went in. The curtains were drawn, the room was dark. In a tumbler on the table a wick in a spoonful of oil was burning with a flickering flame. Josef Blau picked up the light and held it over the cot in which Josef Albert lay. Josef Albert looked at him. The baby's mouth was opened, ready to cry, but Josef Albert did not cry. Did he not cry because the sight of his father frightened and silenced him, or did he recognise him? Josef Blau bent over the cot.

'Josef Albert, my son,' he whispered, 'it's me, we're alone, your father and you, don't be afraid. Don't be frightened, my son, if I bend over you, keep quiet so that no one will come and stop us. Don't be afraid, it's just my teeth chattering, I'm cold, I'm ill, a serious illness, you are my son and heir, oh God, oh God, will you be able to resist it? Can you forgive me for all that? I have to die, Josef Albert, my son, oh, I don't know what name they'll call you by, what should I call you? I want to give you an affectionate name so that you can understand me, even though you are so young. You will wear a sailor suit, like the others, I will not be there to see it, but perhaps a memory of this night will stay with you, a huge, vague memory, and you will understand everything. You see, this is the last time, my son, we are alone, your mother has gone out with the new teacher, Herr Leopold. God knows what is happening, I will never know what has happened but you see, my son, I'm not preventing anything any longer. I pray that you can understand me. It is not for my sake, my son, it is for yours and the others'. Things move with terrible speed from one to the other, it begins with a word, a step, a thought you have had, where did it begin, do you see, I can still see him, he had blond hair and the sun fell on it and now his tongue is swollen and the colour of his face has changed, they say. But perhaps it is not over yet, my son, it will continue, even after I am dead, will go on, to you, my heir, to the others. It is good that I am going to die. Now I will set no new thing in motion. But I want the rest to be over as well, to come to a halt, a stop. All I want is for it to be over, I want a sign that I have been heard, that it will stop, a sign that it will not go on, mercy, mercy for you, for you alone, that the blood will not pour out of your throat, a sign that my prayer has been answered, a sign before I die, do you see, my son, I am praying.'

He put the light on the table and knelt down beside the cot.

'O One and Only, All-powerful Lord – help me, help me, my child, it is farewell, support me, your father, I will not see you again, you will forget me, help me, feel my need of your help, Josef Albert, beloved, in the hour of my death – o Almighty, One and Only, a miracle, o Miraculous One, Miracle-Worker, a sign that it is all over, a sign, o Lord, Lord, Lord.'

He beat his forehead on the floor.

He lay there, unmoving, and waited. He held his breath. His fists were clenched. What was that moving? Was it Josef Albert in his cot? It was as if someone were tossing and turning in bed, and now there was a sigh, a deep, long-drawn-out sigh. Had not Josef Albert's face been old and wrinkled from the very beginning? Josef Blau had not recognised his face. Now he recognised the voice. It came out of the mouth of the grandson, but it was his voice, the voice of the court usher, Josef Blau's father, in whom his life had had its beginning, its origin, nothing died, everything lived, everything continued on its way, like that sigh from the grandfather to the grandson, that was the sign, there was no end, that was the answer given to Josef Blau by God, whose presence he had reached in the hour of his death. At Josef Blau's end his beginning rose up as a plaintive sigh, accusing him.

Josef Blau stood up. He turned away. He did not want to see Josef Albert's face. Perhaps Josef Albert's cheeks were as hollow as those of Josef Blau's mother, perhaps Josef Albert's tongue was already sticking out between his lips, like that of Laub, his pupil. Josef Blau did not want a further sign.

When he went back into the living-room, Selma was standing there before him in her hat and coat. Josef Blau swayed. Selma put her arms round him and took him back to his bed. He was sobbing and she heard him whisper, 'My child, my child,' several times over, as if in sorrowful despair, as if something bad had happened to Josef Albert. She asked him, but he did not hear what she was saying. Now he was in bed, breathing heavily, his face pale and his eyes closed.

Chapter Twelve

Uncle Bobek nodded and waved to Josef Blau, who was sitting at the bottom of the table, between old Hämisch and Modlizki. Uncle Bobek laughed. He toasted his guests and placed his hand on that of Selma's mother, who lowered her eyes and smiled. She was wearing a low-cut, sleeveless dress and had pinned on a rose.

Uncle Bobek ate and talked and laughed. He chomped and slurped, cracked the bones with his teeth and sucked the marrow out of them. Uncle Bobek unbuttoned his waistcoat. He drank to Selma's mother and Josef Blau. He put his beer-mug down and threw his arms out wide.

'Let's all stay together till the break of day, my dear friends. Yes, yes! Let's eat and drink, and in between we'll talk. You won't leave good old Bobek all on his own. Eat your fill and drink your fill, I say, in honour of myself and of Blau, because he's back on his feet again, and of my godchild, or grandchild, since this young lady is his grandmother, I'd never have thought it would turn out like this, but there it is, I don't bear anyone a grudge. My godchild is weak, it gets that from its father, but with God's help it will survive. Why should one not put one's trust in God, I always say? Look at me, I say, I trust in God and I don't bear anyone a grudge. Doesn't everything have a rosy glow when you're eating and drinking?'

First of all they had a glass of corn schnapps, then soup with chicken liver and mushrooms in large, deep bowls. Uncle Bobek cut big hunks of bread into it and dredged them up with his spoon. Then Martha brought in a wooden platter with veal and pork cut up in thick slices on it and bowls of sauerkraut and dumplings. There was a barrel of beer between the two windows. Uncle Bobek had broached it himself. Now they were eating stuffed chicken. Uncle Bobek crunched up the bones and spat them back out onto his plate. At brief intervals he drank a glass of schnapps, opening his mouth wide, leaning back and pouring it down his throat.

Uncle Bobek ate and drank. He laughed, he waved, he slapped his thighs with his little podgy hands.

He gave a blissful sigh as he squashed a particularly tasty morsel against his palate. Everything was bathed in a rosy glow when Uncle Bobek was eating and drinking, thought Josef Blau. God had not overcome Uncle Bobek, not him.

Herr Leopold was sitting between Selma and her mother. He cut up his meat into small pieces and chewed them tirelessly, mouth closed.

'Eat up, eat up, Herr Professor,' said Uncle Bobek. 'You're not keeping up. Oh yes, I know what they say nowadays. Chew each bit on either side of your mouth I don't know how many times. But where would we get with that, I ask? Believe me, Herr Professor, you couldn't eat a third, there wouldn't be time and you'd get tired and full more quickly. You have to get on with it, I say, and enjoy it.'

Herr Leopold did not reply. He was talking to Selma. With all the noise of plates, knives, forks and voices, Josef Blau could not make out what he was saying. But he could see that Selma was smiling. Now the new teacher came to take her out every day. Josef Blau spent the whole day sitting at the window, wrapped up in warm blankets. His temperature went up in the evening and at night his body was damp with cold sweat.

Josef Blau was sitting to the right of Modlizki, at the narrow end of the table, opposite Uncle Bobek. On Josef Blau's right was old Hämisch. Old Hämisch cut the soft bits out of his bread and heaped the crusts up in a pile in front of his plate. Whenever Uncle Bobek raised his glass, he toasted him.

'All the best to you too,' he repeated each time. Then he stared down at his plate in embarrassment.

On Uncle Bobek's left was Pollatschek, who dealt in flour on the commodities market. He was short, bald and a friend of Bobek's since their young days. Pollatschek was wearing a flower in his buttonhole. He spoke in a high, crowing voice. Frau Pollatschek, in a blue silk dress and tightly corseted, was sitting between her husband and old Hämisch. From time to time she would place her hand on Pollatschek's arm and say, in an admonitory whisper, 'Pollatschek!'

Her eyes were small and deep-set, her nose jutted out sharply and her lower lip hung down.

'Just like the good old days, Pollatschek,' said Uncle Bobek, 'isn't that so?' His hand fell heavily on Pollatschek's shoulder. 'Look me in the eye, Pollatschek, old friend, look me in the eye.'

Pollatschek raised his glass. 'Here's to the young couple,' he cried.

They all lifted up their glasses and drank. Herr Leopold stood up and, holding his glass out in front of him, bowed to Uncle Bobek and Selma's mother. He was wearing a black jacket and a black-and-white striped tie with a pearl tie-pin.

'And all of you here,' Uncle Bobek cried, 'you're all so good to me, I know, you've all come, you haven't left me alone, no, no, I thought I might well end up alone this time, they won't come as they did the last time, I thought,' he stared into space with a melancholy expression, 'but here they are, my old friends, you see, they're all sitting there, eating and drinking in my honour. My friends, I say, my friends! We all sat round like this the last time, there were more of them, you can say what you like, Pollatschek, about everything being the same, there were still more of them, but why dwell on that, I say, I ask you? Here we sit, and we're still eating and drinking, let's be content with what we have. Have we changed, Pollatschek? No, no, I say, as God's my witness, I say it's still the same Bobek sitting here as the man who took poor Martha, God rest her soul, the way she looked, a virgin, as true as I hope for God's help in my last hour, I, Bobek, was the first, no one else. But today I don't bear anyone a grudge, no, no, Mathilda dear, you are innocent, it's not you fault, but that doesn't alter the fact that the bride is not the same as the other one, all those years ago. You're the only one who's still the same Pollatschek, there you sit, drinking beer and schnapps, eating soup and veal and chicken, and still leaving the pork, you see, just as you always did.'

'I'm a modern man, Bobek, a freethinker, you know me. But as a . . .'

'Pollatschek!' Frau Pollatschek cried out, blushing. She stared at her plate.

'Why should I keep quiet about it, Rosa? Bobek's my friend and his friends are my friends. I don't believe in anything, Bobek, but I've always stuck to that. For the children's sake if for nothing else. You never know, the Lord will provide, they say, and not everything goes the way you'd like. Is Roubitschek not a freethinker, Bobek? First class, the top man, a VIP, a genius, when he's slept badly the commodities market's dead as a doornail. Let me finish, Bobek. Well, he has children too, three fine boys. A little on the small side, that they get from their mother, God, she's no beauty, but she has a nose for business. And what does he do, the eldest, Adolf he's called? Goes on an outing in the mountains and can't be found, the firm's future vanished without trace. Roubitschek never goes to the synagogue, but now he goes. He stands up and out loud, the whole of the commodities market was there, word had got round, out loud he calls on God, yes, and makes a vow, the top man, it sent shivers down everyone's spine, if his son comes back, his Adolf, he'll change his will, he vows, all the money he has . . .'

'Pollatschek!' Frau Pollatschek warned, putting her hand on his arm. Pollatschek was red in the face, his voice cracked. He shook off his wife's hand.

'All the money he has, I say,' Pollatschek cried, beating his breast, 'millions they put it at, Bobek, if his Adolf comes back, safe and sound, all his money, right down to the last copper, he'll disinherit his own children and leave it to − is he not a great man, Roubitschek − leave it to? To whom? I ask. To Adolf, if he comes back, the others won't get it, only Adolf, his favourite, he's already in the firm. Now you could say Adolf would have come back without the vow. But is that sure? Perhaps the vow helped. So what does Roubitschek do, the genius? Goes round and buys up houses, inns, building plots. Adolf gets the money, the others get the houses. Why should they go empty-handed, his own flesh and blood? Was anyone worse off because he went to the synagogue? Everything's as it should be. Is anyone the worse off if I eat no pork and make up for it with more chicken? You can be as much of a free-thinker as you like, that's something that's best left as it is.'

Uncle Bobek pushed a glass of kümmel over to him. 'Drink,' he said. 'What's the point of telling us about all these customs and traditions? What do I care what vow some Jew made? Cheer me up, Pollatschek, cheer me up. The party hasn't livened up as it did last time.'

'Pollatschek!' Frau Pollatschek warned. She turned to old Hämisch. 'He can't take anything. Not any more. Food or drink . . . a bit of sausage and he lies there the whole night groaning. He ought to do something about it, I tell him, and my eldest keeps going on at him to see a specialist. It costs money, of course it does, but at least you know. But him! You talk to him.'

Old Hämisch gave an embarrassed nod.

Modlizki leant over to Josef Blau. 'If you'll permit me, something's just occurred to me,' he whispered. 'Aren't Blau and Laub the same, if you switch the letters round?'

'What are you after?'

'It just occurred to me. But presumably it's not important.'

Uncle Bobek thumped the table with his fist.

'Don't stop, don't stop. Wine, I say, bring some wine, Martha. When Bobek gives a party nothing's too good or too dear, food and drink. Look me in the eyes, my dear friends, drink to me and talk to me, we're friends, Uncle Bobek is everyone's friend, Uncle Bobek has no enemies, you tell me things and I'll tell you things. There are people, you know, who don't understand. Don't drink, they say, it'll send you to your grave and God won't count it among your good deeds. But I say unto you, the wine grows out of the earth like bread, let us break bread together and take wine, what does that remind me of, I am overcome, don't you see, yes, yes, you feel like crying, like having a good cry, God knows why you suddenly feel like that, but perhaps it's not the worst that can happen when you're suddenly overwhelmed, even if you are a man who's been through a lot, give everyone some, Martha, my child, they will be overcome too, it will loosen their tongues and we'll drink and talk until morning.'

He held up his full glass of wine in his left hand, waved to each in turn with his right and emptied the glass.

Pollatschek held up his glass to the light. He took a mouthful, put his head back and gargled with the wine before he swallowed it.

'Peeeh, peeeh,' he said, swaying his head from side to side in contentment. 'Wine all around.'

Only then did he empty his glass.

What was it Modlizki had whispered to Josef Blau? Now Modlizki stood up. He took the bottle of wine out of Martha's hand and stood respectfully behind Bobek's chair. When Uncle Bobek had emptied his glass, Modlizki stepped forward and filled it again.

Why had Josef Blau not died that evening when he had prayed at Josef Albert's bedside? Why had he woken up again after that night? Why was he here? He wanted to get up and go into the neighbouring room to see Josef Albert, his child. He was a weak child, but one should trust in the Lord. What was the meaning of the two names, oh God, oh God, Deus, Deus meus, quare est tristis anima mea et quare conturbas me? Why is my soul sad, and why, oh why do you cast down my soul?

'Things are not the same as they were, Pollatschek,' said Uncle Bobek. He sighed and gazed mournfully into space. 'No, no. You can say what you like. About thirty people round the table, not counting the lads from Holitz. And here are the nine of us, sitting staring at each other like grave-diggers. At the other wedding people shouted and sang so much you couldn't hear yourself speak, and there wasn't enough of anything, it vanished from the bowls and dishes before you had time to look at it, as true as I'm still the same man I was, and one song after the other, yes, and music you could dance to, I can still see myself, Pollatschek, sitting there clapping my hands and singing along with the tune, it's still going through my head, as I hope for God's help, I couldn't stay on my feet any more, I'd drunk too much, hahaha – God knows what the cause is, but it's not the same as it was then, nothing can be repeated . . .'

Selma's mother had her head in her hands and was crying.

'There she is, Pollatschek, crying like a maiden,' said Uncle Bobek. 'Just you look at her, Pollatschek. Why's she sitting there saying nothing. Drink, I say, sing, I say, music, music, there was music then, Mathilda, why did you forget that? And everything began so beautifully.'

Herr Leopold had stood up. He was holding his wine glass in his hand. Silently he looked round the assembled company.

'Shh, shh,' said Pollatschek.

'I hope you will allow me,' he said, 'to congratulate the young couple, if only in a few brief words. I am unaccustomed to public speaking and I ask you to bear with me. I lift up my glass to Herr Bobek and his newly wedded wife, and to little Josef Albert. I wish him the best a person can have, a healthy mind in a healthy body, mens sana in corpore sano. To the young couple and their grandson.'

He went up to Uncle Bobek who embraced him and gave him two smacking kisses on each cheek.

Herr Leopold kissed Selma's mother's hand.

'Such a refinement, such breeding,' she shouted.

Modlizki took his mouth organ out of his pocket. He stood behind Uncle Bobek and played 'For he's a jolly good fellow.' Uncle Bobek swung his glass, then he turned to Modlizki and gestured to him.

'Play,' he said. 'Who would have thought it, the lad's brought his harmonica with him, what a splendid lad. I have to apologise to him, you know. You can't help feeling afraid when he's around, I always used to say, fair's fair, but I wouldn't like to be at his mercy. Now everything's fine. Come to my arms, my son, bad people have no songs, I was mistaken, come, embrace me and allow me to call you by the familiar *Du*.' He clinked glasses with Modlizki and kissed him on the cheek. 'Oh yes, you see now, Mathilda, when Bobek gives a party everything takes a turn for the better.'

One after the other they all went up to Bobek to clink glasses with him. Each time Uncle Bobek emptied his glass.

After Josef Blau had drunk to him, Uncle Bobek grasped Blau's left hand, which was hanging down.

'There you are, there you are. I don't hold it against you, even if it wasn't so urgent. But drink, drink, wine stimulates the blood, I always say, and that's what you need, Blau, blood, blood, I tell you, blood, so you've got some to spare if you have another of your attacks.'

Modlizki went on playing. Uncle Bobek clapped his hands and swayed to and fro so that his chair started to wobble. Now Modlizki was playing a march. Leaning on the table, Uncle Bobek stood up and marched up and down in the empty space between the windows and the table, wheezing and swaying.

'Let's dance. Play something we can dance to, my son.'

Modlizki played a six-step. In a coquettish pose, hands on hips, Uncle Bobek turned to the right and the left. Everyone stood up. Martha and Pollatschek moved the chairs to the side. Josef Blau was standing leaning on the table. He saw Herr Leopold put his arms round Selma's waist. Selma lifted up her long skirt with her left hand and pulled it tight round her legs. She was swinging round and round with Herr Leopold, her eyes closed tight, her head leant back. Behind them Uncle Bobek, holding a glass with the wine sloshing over the rim at every step, was hopping from one foot to the other, gurgling and shouting.

'With me, with me, my daughter, look at her, my daughter, with me now.'

Selma did not hear him.

'Enough,' she said.

Herr Leopold led her to a chair. She sank onto it and held on tight to the seat with both hands. She kept her eyes shut and was smiling. A lock of hair had come loose and fallen down over her forehead. Herr Leopold stood beside her. 'Drink, drink. Give her some wine, I say,' cried Uncle Bobek. 'Drink, Selma, my daughter, drink. What next, Modlizki, what next?'

'Perhaps someone should make a speech. Perhaps Herr Blau, he would be the man for it.'

'Bravo, bravo! He's to make a speech. He's the man for it.' Uncle Bobek collapsed onto the sofa. 'Come and sit over here, Pollatschek, beside me. And Blau's to make a speech, I say.'

Uncle Bobek had put his arm round Pollatschek's shoulders. Modlizki poured some wine into the glass he had in his hand. Uncle Bobek put the glass to his lips. His hand was trembling, making the wine spill over his jacket.

'Give him something to drink, Modlizki. It loosens the tongue, I always say. A glass of wine . . . that's it, my boy, that's it . . . and a schnapps . . . now off you go, off you go, my boy.'

Josef Blau did not resist. He drank the drinks Modlizki handed him, the wine and the schnapps. He held on tight to the back of the chair.

Selma stood before him, her eyes aglow. 'Speak,' she said, 'you must speak too, do you hear?'

She stepped back. Now she was standing next to Herr Leopold by the wall with the windows. But someone had grasped Josef Blau by the arm. It was old Hämisch, Josef Blau recognised him by his voice.

'I am just a guest here and that's very nice of you, Herr Bobek,' old Hämisch said. 'I'm an old man and when Herr Bobek said, "I'm getting married, you mustn't miss the wedding," well, I've known you all for a long time and I've always thought Frau Kosterhoun and Herr Bobek would make a match one of these days. Why ever not? Why ever not? And why shouldn't I be there, I thought?'

Old Hämisch broke off. It was as if he expected an answer. No one spoke. Old Hämisch cleared his throat. He was still holding onto Josef Blau's arm.

'Yes, yes,' said old Hämisch softly, staring down at the floor in front of him.

'Quite right,' Uncle Bobek shouted.

'It's because there was talk of a speech, Herr Bobek, begging your pardon. I just thought, well . . . even if I'm just a guest, and if they listen to me . . . But no offence meant, far be it from me, I'm a God-fearing man and as Herr Pollatschek said, "That's something that's best left as it is," he said. But the Herr Professor is ill, isn't he, there's beads of sweat on his brow,

145

just as there were with my daughter, if he gets worked up he might start coughing blood again.'

'Who's saying he's to get worked up, Herr Hämisch. Nothing of the sort. If he says nothing it puts a damper on the mood of the party, you see, and that's why we're gathered here, isn't it? Or am I wrong? Why's he not saying anything? Everyone says he should speak, but he's not speaking. Perhaps it'll help him make up his mind if you sit down, Herr Hämisch. Give him a drink, Modlizki.'

Old Hämisch let go of Josef Blau's arm. Head bowed, he went back to the wall and sat down.

'To the young couple,' Pollatschek shouted.

'Certainly,' said Bobek. 'Why not? Make a speech to the young couple, as far as I'm concerned.'

Josef Blau looked at Selma beside Herr Leopold. They seemed to be a long way away, as if he were looking at them through the wrong end of a pair of opera glasses. Was Herr Leopold still holding her? Was he still embracing her?

'Oh yes,' said Josef Blau, 'Everyone knew, from the very beginning we all knew. The young couple. But you couldn't stand in their way. No one knows how it's all going to end.'

'He's right you know, Pollatschek,' said Uncle Bobek. 'Don't you see, he's right. No one knows how it's all going to end. Go on, keep talking.'

Josef Blau took a step towards Selma and Herr Leopold. He stretched out his hand.

'Go on, give each other a kiss. Why aren't you giving each other a kiss?'

His voice was loud. He held his hand outstretched and pointed at Selma and Herr Leopold with his index finger.

'Blau!' Selma exclaimed. She sank onto a chair and held her hands over her ears. 'Stop it, stop it, stop it,' she cried.

'He's drunk,' said Selma's mother.

Herr Leopold went up to Josef Blau. 'That's enough,' he said.

'The happy couple.' Josef Blau nodded his head. Herr Leopold took him by the shoulder, turned Josef Blau round and urged him towards the door to the bedroom. Josef Blau did not resist. Selma jumped up. She threw herself between Herr Leopold and Josef Blau and tried to push Herr Leopold back.

'Let go of him!' she cried. 'At once! Don't touch him, I tell you.'

'I'm sorry,' said Herr Leopold. He bowed to Selma and went slowly back to the window.

'You are ridiculous, Blau,' said Uncle Bobek. 'No, no, Pollatschek, that's not the same as it was. Give me a schnapps, Modlizki.'

Josef Blau went into the bedroom. He closed the door carefully behind him. No one had followed him. He sat beside Josef Albert, who was sleeping. A nightlight was flickering wearily on the table, throwing swaying shadows onto the wall. From the next room came the sound of Uncle Bobek's loud voice. What was that about the letters, if you switched them round? Did they have to be each other's fate, the teacher and the pupil, just for the banal reason that their names were the same? Was a name more than just a sound, was it part of a person, could you not have a different one and be the same person? Were you attached to your name, or was your name attached to you? Was this his wife, this his son and were these his pupils because he was Josef Blau, or was he Josef Blau because this was his wife, this his son and these his pupils? If he had died by his own hand while he was still at school, would he then have been Laub or would it have been Blau who had died as a schoolboy? If he, Josef Blau, had been born as the second child of his parents, would he then have been Josef Blau's brother and have died in infancy? In that case who would have been Josef Blau, or would Josef Blau not have existed? Am I not just one single individual, Josef Blau asked himself, who only appears once in time, and have I just one, single fate, for which I am responsible, or could I have many names and many fates? Could I take on the fate of my pupil Laub, continue it, atone for it, put it right? What is the connection between all this, what does it signify? The more one thought about it, the more confusing it became.

147

Now Modlizki was playing another dance on his mouth organ. Perhaps Selma was dancing with Herr Leopold again and everyone was watching and laughing. The door opened. Someone came in and shut it behind them again. Josef Blau kept his head bowed.

'Uncle Bobek is right,' said Selma. She was standing right in front of Josef Blau. Her voice sounded harsh. 'You are ridiculous.'

She sat down on the bed.

Josef Blau did not reply.

'What do you want? Oh God, don't you understand that I love you, only you? I watch by your bedside, and here, look, the child is our child and still you don't trust me.'

She stood up. She went up to him and put her arm round his shoulders.

'What is it you think? Do you think I love Herr Leopold? He looks after me. I'm worried, about you among other things . . . but . . . but . . .'

She took her arm away.

'Do you want me to swear to you,' she cried, 'there . . .' she pointed at Josef Albert's cot, 'by his life?'

'Be quiet,' he begged.

'Haha, you wouldn't believe me, even then. What have I done? No other woman would have done it . . . I wear long skirts like an old woman, but you won't believe me . . . What else, tell me, what else do you want that will make you believe me?'

He did not move.

She took a step back. She fixed her eyes on him, sitting there before her, slumped down, his face in his hands. She stayed like that for a moment, then she leant her head back.

'I know,' she said softly. 'You were going to say it once, but then . . . you said something else. I knew what you wanted. Right . . . it will be done, the thing you wanted.'

'I do not want anything, Selma.'

'It will be done. Then you won't be able to go on thinking I have secret rendezvous with Herr Leopold or with . . . Karpel.'

148

'How did you find out about the bill of exchange?'

'Modlizki told me. I had to promise I wouldn't tell anyone it was him who told me. He said the child would be cursed if I told anyone. But Herr Leopold says that's silly. If you don't believe me, ask Bobek who had the bill of exchange. He paid it off today. My mother wouldn't give him the money until today.'

'Who had it?'

'Berger, the man who lent Bobek the money.'

'No, no,' said Josef Blau.

'Berger had it. Ask Bobek, ask my mother, ask anyone.'

No, no, thought Josef Blau, it cannot be true. It must not be true. Why else would I have gone to Kasernengasse? Deus, Deus meus!

Selma's mother opened the door. She called Selma. In the next room the guests were saying goodbye.

Uncle Bobek was sitting on the sofa. Selma's mother was standing next to him, filling his glass.

'They've left me, they've all left me. It's not the same as it was,' he said mournfully. 'No, no, it's not like that, they've left me in the lurch, I have no one I can look in the eye, no one, no friend, old Bobek's alone and . . . and . . . yes, yes . . . old Bobek's not ashamed of his tears.'

The tears were running down Bobek's cheeks.

Selma's mother bent down over him.

'You're not alone, Bobek,' she shouted, 'I'm with you and I'll stay with you, my darling.'

'Shut up!' said old Bobek, his voice choked with tears, and pushed her away from him.

Chapter Thirteen

The sound of the boys' voices coming from the classrooms was like the muffled roar of a distant river. Sometimes, when a door opened briefly to admit a late pupil, it rose and flooded the tiled floor of the bare corridor. It was a few minutes to eight. Tight knots of boys stood round those who had prepared their lessons and were reading out the translation of the set passages. Sitting at their desks, they rocked to and fro, muttering vocabulary, slapping their foreheads to stop the words escaping, swopping cribs and hurriedly writing out in their exercise books the homework they had neglected to do at home.

Herr Leopold went up to his colleague Blau. He shook his hand. He offered to accompany him to the class, but Josef Blau declined. Herr Leopold handed over a notebook bound in black. It contained the names of the pupils in alphabetical order and alongside each name an assessment of the pupil's performance during the time Herr Leopold had been taking the class.

Josef Blau hesitated for a moment before opening the door. Would the shouts die away when he entered, would they submit, sitting at their desks, look at him in silence, or would the rebellion that would sweep him away break out immediately? He opened the door. The boys stood up, then sat down in silence at his sign. He did not look at the class. He felt their eyes on him, testing, probing, piercing, shameless eyes rummaging round inside him, curious eyes that missed nothing, neither a new line that had etched itself on his face, nor a different, more hesitating step, nor a changed heartbeat.

As before, Josef Blau went straight from the door up onto the dais and followed his usual path to his seat. He signed his initials in the class register. There they sat, just as he had left them, at their desks, one beside the other in the prescribed order, motionless, looking at him, all of them but one. Josef Blau lowered his eyes. There was a yawning gap, an open mouth screaming accusation at him. They had not occupied the desk. They wanted him to fill the gap he had made. There was Karpel, his head bowed over his desk. Karpel had told them how it had all happened. Josef Blau could not see his face, which perhaps had a smile on it, only the line of white scalp in his parting. He could not leave the desk empty. He must fill the gap, block up the screaming mouth. He must arrange for another boy to sit at the desk. He had thought about what he had to say, for he had expected this.

'Vacha,' he intended to say, 'sit at Laub's desk.'

But Josef Blau kept his head bowed and did not say it. The class waited in silence. He could not see the boys, but he could feel that they had understood. The rigid postures relaxed, boys looked at each other, nodded to each other. They felt that they could stand up now and he would put up no resistance, that he would no longer hold them, compel them, for they sensed what he had recognised. They sensed that it seemed too much for him, sitting there, head bowed, silent. For that too could set things in motion, that too combined with the boys, that too led them, or led them astray, and one could not say where it would end.

A chair was moved. Josef Blau looked up. Bohrer had stood up. What did Bohrer want? Was he the first to rise, while the others were still hesitating? Was he going to come up to him now, to the laughter of the rest of the class, and pat the teacher on the shoulder with his red, frost-swollen hands? The boy came slowly to the front, arms dangling, unsure of himself. He did not look at his teacher. He stopped at the front row and sat down in Laub's empty seat, opposite Josef Blau. He put his hands on the desk in front of him and kept his head bowed. Oh, the others had realised that Bohrer had got up to save his teacher, that they were connected, Bohrer, the pupil, the son of a clerk with shiny patches on his jacket sleeves, and Josef Blau. Weren't they smiling? Oh God, how long would it be until this lesson was over? There was one of them bending down to have a furtive look at his watch under the desk.

Josef Blau did not go to his usual place by the window. Sitting at his desk, he opened the book and, without looking up, began to read where Herr Leopold had left off. Now they would be comparing his voice with Herr Leopold's full, rich voice. They loved the other teacher, just as everyone loved him, as Selma loved him, her mother, even Uncle Bobek. The other teacher, who had no sense of the responsibility he was burdening himself with when he stood in front of the class. Herr Leopold had not been given a sign, God had not chosen him to be one who understood. If signs had been vouchsafed him, Herr Leopold had not understood them.

Josef Blau asked questions. The boys answered, but their answers were hesitant, uncertain in tone, diffident. It was as if they first had to reassure themselves that this was real: the teacher's gaze, which usually kept them taut with apprehension, fixed on the floor, his quiet voice, almost turning his questions into pleas, no cunningly thought-out new plan to subject them once more, thoroughly and finally, to the tight rein of discipline. The longer the lesson went on, the louder and more assured the boys' voices became. One voice sparked off another, one took over the tone of another, exaggerating it, feeling for the limit to which they could go without the teacher rising and putting down the rebellion. Josef Blau did not turn his gaze on the boys he called on to answer questions. Let what had been set in motion come. Let the boys see what they already suspected, namely that they were the stronger, the victors. That he could no longer stand in their way of setting new things in motion, could no longer stand in front of them to compel them with all his might, to keep them frozen in motionlessness, at a distance.

He put no questions to Bohrer or Karpel. Karpel stared at the open book in front of him. He was the one Josef Blau had seen last, a shadow beside Modlizki in the dark street on the night when Modlizki had called up to him, the night that had begun so propitiously. Karpel knew more than the others. He knew why the blood had poured out of their teacher's throat. He had seen their teacher in the yellow light of the street-lamp, his coat collar turned up, his hat pulled down over his eyes, as Laub cried out, perhaps had watched him as he hurried off, until the black gate of the barracks hid him from view. Now Karpel was sitting there in silence. But he was thinking about it, and he knew what had happened at Uncle Bobek's wedding, there was much that he knew, that Herr Leopold came to see Selma every day and sat with her in the living-room while Josef Blau shut himself away in the room that had been Selma's mother's, for Josef Blau did not stand in the way. Modlizki would have told him, for they would certainly still meet as they used to and Modlizki would fill the boy with his hatred of the teacher he was pursuing, impossible to say why, but he stuck to him like a leech, never letting go, as a lover cannot let go of his bride, nothing satisfied Modlizki. But was not everything over now? Josef Blau no longer stopped things happening, no longer provoked, no longer burdened himself with blame, unless it was by still breathing, doing and saying what was absolutely necessary to live, to feed Josef Albert. Oh, even that was too much, that he stood there, tied to so many fates, responsible for the path they took, whether he acted or restricted his actions, that he was still tied to Josef Albert, dragged him down into his own fate, for what happened to Josef Blau must also happen to Josef Albert. When the boys went home they would tell each other what each had seen for himself. Modlizki would encourage them. And tomorrow they were bound to rise up against him, cruelly, without pity, against him who did not resist, to bring shame upon him, to destroy him and thus Josef Albert as well, the child Josef Blau had fathered, the child to whom he had passed on everything, himself, his father, his mother, sickness, guilt and entanglement. It was not right that Josef Blau should presume to teach, he must stop doing it, stop setting himself up as leader, as judge. There was a dead body on his path. It was not right that he did not separate his path from all other paths. He must go away, to solitude, as a labourer with a farmer, as a beggar on the road, alone, without Selma, without a child, forget his child so that his thoughts did not take hold of it, not be to blame for anyone's fate any more, not add any more to what he was to blame for, the consequences of which continued without end.

He sat at the table opposite Selma. Selma had bound up her head in a tight-fitting black scarf that went from her forehead, over her ears and round the back of her neck. She had shaved her head so that she would not attract men and to make him believe her. He did not look at her. He avoided her eye. She asked how it had been at school, whether the talking was tiring, whether he felt well. His answers were brief and friendly. After the meal he stood up. He went into the room that Selma's mother used to have. He sat there, wrapped up in a blanket, and looked out of the window at the tangle of rails at the station. The room had a separate door onto the staircase. Josef Blau listened to every noise that could be heard on the stairs. The stairs creaked. But it was someone going to see the neighbours. Then steps going away again. But that now must be Herr Leopold. He took two steps at a time. Now he was at the top and ringing the bell. Selma opened the door to him and he came in, talking loudly. The sound of their voices was muffled, for the doors of Josef Albert's room, which was between him and them, were closed. Now he could not hear anything. Were they talking quietly? Or had they stopped talking, were holding each other mutely in their arms? He did not get up, he did not go into the room.

Again there were steps on the stairs. Someone blew his nose at the door. A match was struck. Now someone was feeling the door to the room where Josef Blau was sitting. Josef Blau opened it. Outside was a man with a parcel.

'Does Professor Blau live her?' he asked. In his hand he had a round, blue cap such as messenger boys for the department stores wear.

'I am he.'

'I'm to deliver this.'

Josef Blau took the parcel from the man. He signed for the delivery in a notebook the man handed him. The man went back down the stairs.

Josef Blau took the parcel over to the window. It was a large, rectangular package wrapped in white paper. Josef Blau undid the knot and removed the wrapping. Before him lay a brown cardboard box with a large, square piece of white paper stuck to the lid. On the paper was written – in large block capitals, presumably to disguise the handwriting – the one word: Theresa.

Josef Blau closed his eyes. This was it. What he had foreseen had happened. Nothing could hold the boys back any more. Should he open it? Should he see what they had sent him? Should he put the parcel in the stove and burn it, without seeing what it contained? It was better to know, to understand the path they were taking, not in order to oppose them, but to prepare his heart for everything that was in store for him.

He took off the lid. Perhaps, he thought with a smile, it contains a bomb. I open it and I have found the path. But the parcel was light and they were not thinking of killing him, they wanted him alive, to hound him as the huntsmen do a fox.

He took off the lid. He saw coloured silk. He picked it up and was bemused: a lace-trimmed, pink silk petticoat, like the ones Selma and her mother had. How could they know about that? They could not have got it from Modlizki, no, no, one of them had seen her in this petticoat. He dropped it back into the box, put the box in the cupboard and locked it. He leant his forehead against the window-pane and closed his eyes. His face was burning. What was this? What did they want?

Selma opened the door. He did not turn round. He did not want her to see his face, red with shame.

'Herr Leopold's here,' she said. 'Won't you come? The coffee's on the table.'

'Thank you, I . . . I think I have to go out for a short while.'

When she had left the room, he took his hat and went out.

He came back an hour later. He climbed the stairs carefully, he did not want them to hear him coming. The sound of voices came from the apartment. Herr Leopold must still be there. Perhaps Selma's mother had come round too. He opened the door to his room quietly and lit the light. Then he opened the cupboard where he had put the box and placed next to it another, similar one he had been carrying under his arm, locked the cupboard again and sat down at the table.

Since he could not find any writing paper, nor a pen and ink, he tore a page out of his notebook and took a pencil out of his pocket. He wrote:

'The cupboard in your mother's room is not empty, as you think it is. There are two boxes in it. One has 'Theresa' written on it. It contains a new, lace-trimmed, pink silk petticoat and was sent to 'Theresa', as you know my pupils call me. They sent it, they want to destroy me, for the petticoat is exactly the same as the one you have and only someone who has seen you wearing it can have chosen it. But that is not what I wanted to write about. Where would it lead us? I have decided not to to question you, to press you for an answer. I will never know what happens when you go out for a walk with Herr Leopold. Whatever you swear, I will not know in the same way as if I were there. I believe what reason tells me, but I will no longer stand in your way. You have shaved your head and I thought, like that she would not expose herself to any man, but perhaps that is the very thing that drives you into their arms, the fact that I could make such a demand, since even before I expressed it, you knew that I demanded it. But even if I had not made any demands and had done something different, if I had begged you, if I had said that I loved you, perhaps it would have been that which drove you into their arms, one never knows what a word can lead to. But I was not going to talk about that box, but about the other one. You can keep the petticoat for your own use or give it to your mother, who likes wearing that kind of thing, or do whatever you like with it.

The contents of the other box are for Josef Albert. When he is bigger and is going to school, open the box and take out one of the suits in it. Both suits are of the same type. One is for a six-year-old boy, the other somewhat bigger. They are blue sailor suits with light blue collars, white ties and short trousers decorated with gold buttons at the bottom. They are made from good, hard-wearing material, I chose them carefully myself from a reputable store.

I do not know when the situation will arise in which this letter will be found, but at least I have made provision for it, since it is my wish that my son should wear these suits when he goes to school. If the circumstances, for which these lines are intended, should arise now or in the near future, then I will never have heard my son speak my name. I love him, but what is the point of talking about it? It is hard for me to tear myself away from him, not to be with him any more, not to feel his warmth, not to see his gaze, so full of premonition. Perhaps his eye will search for his father. If I did not love him so much, I would have stayed with him.

I think all this will be a mystery to you. I am not more guilty than other men, but I have been chosen to see my guilt. I would bear it, if the retribution were to fall on me alone, but it falls on everyone, for we are all connected with each other.'

He wanted to go on and explain this to her, to talk about the judge who recorded their transgressions and before whom they were as one, a class like the boys at school; about the way things followed, one on top of the other, word on word, step on step; about his struggles to find the way to God and about the sign he had been given. But he felt he could not say it. He took the piece of paper and put it in his pocket.

Chapter Fourteen

Discipline was in tatters. They had stood up, singly and in groups, they were laughing, shouting, uttering mocking, insulting words, saying things to spur the others on, they whistled, they thumped their desks, growing louder and less restrained with every second, first of all individual cries, then all together, mouths wide open, hair dishevelled, faces flushed. One swept the other along with him, their voices cracked and screeched, they were all in the grip of a wild excitement as they cast off the discipline their teacher had imposed on them, saw order swept away, the order he had maintained because he knew what was bound to happen if it went, the equilibrium of forces, the dominant power of the teacher, saw him, Josef Blau, their teacher, sitting there, weak, helpless, acquiescent, doing nothing, his hands over his eyes, his face bent over his desk. They were no longer bound together in alphabetical order, Blum to Bohrer, Christian, Drapal, Fischer, Fleischer, Fuchs, Glaser, Goldmann, Haber, Japp, Karpel, Lebenhardt, Müller, Pazofski, Reis, Vacha, no longer bound to their seats, everything had been swept away, they stood up, they laughed, they mocked, the unusual situation confused them, they did not know how to take best advantage of it. Now they were throwing paper darts at him.

He could distinguish voices. He did not look up, but he recognised them. Pazofski's, already a manly bass, Lebenhardt's feminine squeals, Japp's bleating laughter. But where was Karpel? Was he not crying out, not laughing with the others? Josef Blau could not hear Karpel's voice. He would have recognised it among all the others. Was Karpel a mute commander directing the attack? Karpel was silent? Perhaps everything was not yet lost. Perhaps if Josef Blau stood up and calmly, his eyes fixed on the boys, called them to order, addressing the boys by their names and thus catching, cornering, holding them, he could ward off the rebellion, put it down. Perhaps all it needed was a look from him to bring them back to their senses, to make them look at each other, as if in a mirror where they saw their own faces, distorted, a crazed look in their eyes, hair stuck to their foreheads. Perhaps one look would silence the wild cries, turn the ecstatic excitement into embarrassed realisation of what they were doing.

Josef Blau did not stand up. He did not take his hands away from his face. He did not want to put things off any more. He no longer sought mitigation, postponement. He waited. Paper crumpled up into balls, folded into darts struck him, bounced off him. Solid objects were not being thrown yet. Perhaps they would soon start throwing their textbooks at him, inkwells, knives. Their anger was spurred on by his weakness, the sole cause of their anger. He had the feeling they had left their places, were coming to the front of the classroom. Now a voice came from the first row, from Laub's place. It was Bohrer's voice. The others took up the chant, repeated it, at first disjointedly, then in rhythm, stamping their feet, thumping the desks with their fists:

'Murderer, murderer, mur . . . der . . . er!'

I will stand up, thought Josef Blau. I will leave the classroom. I will not resist if they fall on me. I will stand up.

He felt that he was already standing up, felt that his legs were moving. He had also shut the class register, had not forgotten to clamp it underneath his arm as always, had taken his hat. Now he was standing in front of the blackboard facing the class. He had been wrong. They were all sitting at their desks. Was Laub's place empty again? No, Bohrer was sitting in Laub's place. But there was a gap yawning. It was Karpel's place that was empty. Had Karpel not come? The boys looked at their teacher. They were silent. They were expecting something of him, expecting him to say something, do something. But he said nothing. He left, his face turned towards them as if he still thought he could hold them with his gaze, describing his accustomed semi-circle from the dais to the door, he was leaving, there was no doubt about that, he already had the door-knob in his hand and was opening the door. He went out into the corridor, closing the door behind him as carefully as if there were someone asleep in the room he was leaving.

Josef Blau stood still, leaning with his back against the door-frame. All was quiet in the classroom. Now they would be standing behind the door, discussing what to do. They could not believe he had fled for good like that, unresisting, giving in to the first attack. He heard the classroom door being quietly opened from the inside and immediately closed again. They had seen him. Now Josef Blau could hear their voices once more, muted, whispering. They must think he was gathering his strength, waiting until their excitement had died down in order to return after a few minutes. Now they would be preparing a new reception for him. Perhaps they were standing waiting for him in a semi-circle round the door, in order to fall on him violently, at once, from all sides. He would have to disappoint them. He was not going back. He closed his eyes for a moment. He was gathering his strength, they were right about that, but not in order to confront them again. He was going. He would not see them again in their low-cut sailor-suits. Not Karpel. Not Lebenhardt, not one of them. He was leaving all this, without looking back, and Selma and Josef Albert, without farewell, never to return, to be alone, a solitary fate, a solitary life, not linked to others, unburdened by deadly responsibility, no more to entangle Josef Albert, Selma, the boys. He would be a pilgrim, a beggar, a labourer on quiet farms, poor, chaste, obedient and simple in thought, no longer guilty. His thoughts would die and no longer go to Josef Albert. He would stand by the road like a tree. Breathing, smiling, all sin taken away from him, his head clear, clear of Laub, clear of Modlizki, clear of school, of the teacher, clear of wife and child. Birds nest in his hair. His steps are innocent, for no one is entangled in his fate and God, sitting at the long table with the crucifix, has raised His index finger, not to threaten him, but to wave to him. They all have their heads bowed, the boys, Selma, Modlizki, even Uncle Bobek is silent and Selma's mother is smiling, as if she has understood what a beautiful, soft voice is saying or singing. It is the sound of this voice which touches the heart, for the words pass away, the sound is redemption, salvation, so imbued with sweet emotion that the warm tears run down Josef Blau's cheeks.

A hand was gently placed on Josef Blau's shoulder. 'Compose yourself.'

Josef Blau opened his eyes. Herr Leopold was standing in front of him.

'I was in the corridor, I heard everything. It's not that bad, Herr Blau, compose yourself. Certainly, who would have expected that? But you must keep calm. You will see, it is an interlude that will deepen your relationship – yes, really, I mean it seriously – with your pupils. I would like to accompany you, Herr Blau, I will go with you to the class, if you will permit me. You go back as if to say, Right, boys, that's enough of these silly games, let's start playing at school again, shall we? Am I not right? Isn't that the best?'

'I thank you,' said Josef Blau.

'Are you happy with that, Herr Blau? Don't imagine it will weaken your position if I accompany you. A word of explanation, that will do. Or I will stay outside. It's not really necessary for me to accompany you. The boys are already regretting what has happened, no doubt about that, and they'll make up for it. I think the boys in your class are basically good boys. So, if you're ready, in you go.'

'I'm not going back, Herr Leopold.'

'Not going back? What do you mean? Are you going to make a report? Request leave? Don't do that, Herr Blau. Or do it, if you like, but only after you have got through the lesson successfully. Come,' said Herr Leopold, 'permit me to stop you making an irreparable mistake. You will thank me for it, I know you will, Herr Blau. Come.'

He took Josef Blau by the arm, pushed him towards the door and opened it.

The boys were sitting at their desks. They stood up when the door opened. Josef Blau hesitated.

'Go on,' whispered Herr Leopold behind him, 'go on.'

Josef Blau took a step forward. Now he was in the classroom. The boys did not move. Their heads were turned half towards him. Herr Leopold was right. Of course the pupils regretted the incident, they were grateful to him for coming back without having gone to the principal for support in taking strict measures. He would follow Herr Leopold's advice and return to his place as if nothing had happened, continue the lesson, perhaps say a few words at the end, that he had been ill and knew he could count on the support of the class.

The class was still standing. Josef Blau gave the sign to sit down. They hesitated. Now he turned, as always, to go from the door onto the dais. His eye fell on the blackboard. Fixed to it was a large piece of brown paper with a drawing on it and some writing in large letters, like a poster. Josef Blau caught his breath. He did not understand. Were the boys not giggling? It was a female body, large, unclothed, with huge bosom, broad hips, bowed head – that head! The head was shaven, bare, ugly, like a shining sphere. Josef Blau read the words. He closed his eyes. He did not understand. He repeated them quietly:

'Blau's victim Selma.'

He felt for support behind him, the register dropped to the floor. He rushed to the blackboard. He grabbed the drawing, crumpled it up, tore it to pieces. He turned round. The door was still open. Herr Leopold had stayed out in the corridor. Josef Blau could not see him. The boys had not sat down. Their heads were bowed. Surely they were smiling. He went towards them, step by step, he came down from the dais, slowly, mouth open, hands raised with fingers spread, towards the front row. There they sat, with their hair neatly brushed, their nails with white half-moons, their short trousers leaving the flesh of their legs visible and their shirts plunging to a point and revealing their bare necks, they did not move, whose neck was it he was clutching in his fingers so that he could feel the blood throbbing, he saw the whites of the eyes enlarge, the face go red, the mouth open wide. Now they had surrounded him, they were pulling at his arms. He would not let go. They were tearing at his jacket, his sleeves. His hands held the neck tight. That was Herr Leopold talking to him.

162

He was squeezing his wrists so that all the strength drained out of Josef Blau and his fingers let go. He saw the face of the boy leaning back. It was Japp, now he recognised him. The others were holding Japp under his shoulders. They lowered him to the floor. Herr Leopold bent over Japp. Josef Blau heard Herr Leopold's voice. The others stood round Herr Leopold. They formed a circle. They did not see Josef Blau. Josef Blau was alone. He kept his head bowed. The door was open. Slowly he walked out. No one turned to watch him leave.

He walked slowly, straight ahead, not heading anywhere in particular. His heart was pounding, he felt he would soon not be able to go any farther, there was a great pain weighing on his heart like a heavy burden. That is the farewell, he thought. He kept thinking that, it was a moving thought and the emotion eased his pain, bringing tears which were like a soft caress.

He sat down on a bench in the park, resting his head in his hands. That was the farewell. They would search for him in the morning. They would find his letter in the drawer. Selma would cry and put on black clothes. They would assume he was dead because they did not understand him. In his way Uncle Bobek would try to cheer Selma up. Herr Leopold would take Josef Blau's place publicly and soon the memory of Josef Blau would have faded away, just occasionally at night it would come over Selma like a nightmare spirit and over Josef Albert like an incomprehensible, formless dream. Modlizki would come and, completely unmoved, as if he were recounting some everyday happening, report the events of his last class in school. For even now Modlizki would not let go of him. He would sense where he had gone, picking up his trail as a dog sniffs out that of a wounded deer. Even now he was still trying to destroy him, to avenge himself, yes, yes, to avenge himself, that was it, he was avenging himself on Josef Blau, he was the bringer of vengeance, there was no escape, he was the devil, why did children shrink back from him, had not Josef Albert cried out in his cot when Modlizki came in? He had delivered Selma up to them, cleared the way for them with threats that he would destroy Josef Blau, destroy the child, there was no doubt, they had seen her, naked, they had proved their virility with her, perhaps she had smiled as she yielded to them, to Karpel or to several, for they were young, their skin was warm and felt delicate and full of life, they had the virility of youth, they had undone the scarf, exposed the naked, shorn head. Josef Blau should have suspected it when she confronted him at Bobek's wedding, when she danced with Herr Leopold, when Josef Blau made his speech, he was ridiculous, Uncle Bobek had said, she hated him as he gave his speech, as she cut off her hair. Modlizki had seen this and now he was driving her, urging her on until she complied. Modlizki would pursue him and not stop until he had found him. There was no escape, Modlizki was after him, as long as Modlizki was on his scent he would beat him, and if he could not find him, he would find others, Josef Albert, the child! Modlizki's revenge must not continue, must be over once and for all. Josef Blau would not save anything by fleeing, it would continue, even if he left, the wild beast must be satisfied, it wanted him, Josef Blau, here he was, here, here!

'Here I am, here I am,' he whispered. 'Kill me, here I am.'

He stood up.

He wanted to face him, head bowed so Modlizki could split it! That was his goal, that was the end. That was the circle closing. Only now did he realise that Modlizki was the messenger, sent for him, to put an end to him.

He hurried through the park, turning off down the path to where Modlizki lived.

The sacrificial victim, he thought. Someone will give me a white blindfold. Camillus, the attendant at the sacrifice, he thought.

That was the circle closing. Only now did he see that Modlizki was the instrument, the messenger, sent for him, to put an end to him.

He pressed the bell. The door clicked open. He smiled when he saw the white goddess with her gracefully raised arm. She was shining in the bright sun and he felt as if she were looking at him, as if she smiled when he greeted her.

Chapter Fifteen

The hall with the weapons and the stuffed animal heads was not dark as it usually was. The curtains were raised and the daylight was streaming in through the large windows. Nor was Modlizki wearing his black coat. He had a white-and-blue-striped work jacket on and was holding a duster. Now he bowed. Josef Blau had prepared what he was going to say. 'Here I am, kill me,' he had intended to say. But now Modlizki was looking at him with respectful deference, as if awaiting an order. Josef Blau remained silent.

'An unusual time,' said Modlizki.

He placed a chair for Josef Blau. Josef Blau did not sit down. After a pause, Modlizki went on, 'The warm season is beginning. It is advisable to protect articles of clothing and furs with camphor and newspaper. It is a tried and trusted method, as far as we can tell, I might add.'

'What's all this, Modlizki?' said Josef Blau. 'You know why I've come. I've quitted the school. You must have given them the idea, it can't have been anyone else. You wheedled it out of Selma's mother, or Uncle Bobek. Karpel wouldn't have dared on his own, even if he knew. You hate me, Modlizki. What more do you want from me? Speak, speak. What do you want to drive me to?'

'I don't understand,' said Modlizki.

'You don't understand? Must I put it in words of one syllable? They made a drawing of her, hahaha, naked, with shorn head, and hung the picture on the blackboard. You must have told them, you and no one else.'

'Can it only have been me?'

Josef Blau leant on the arm of the chair beside him. 'You're right,' he said in a low voice, 'they could have . . . perhaps they knew it without you . . . but making a drawing, Modlizki, that was your idea, don't deny it, Modlizki . . . you hate me, hate everyone, everyone, yes, but for me you have a special hatred. I always wanted to talk about it, atone for it, perhaps I'm not entirely without blame, I thought, but it would have made no difference. I've not forgotten the look you gave me, at Wismuth's – how long ago was it – when they came to fetch me and left you in the kitchen. You have never forgotten it, when you talk to me that is all that is in your mind, that they left you in the kitchen and invited me to eat off a linen cloth with them. That's what it is, I know, Modlizki, that is why you are seeking revenge, but how long will it go on for, Modlizki, look at me, I'm ready to atone for everything, forget it, it was so long ago, we were children, it's time to bring it to an end.'

Not a muscle moved in Modlizki's face. 'Wismuth?' he said. 'I remember vaguely. A merchant with a little goatee and a round belly. I thought it was at Herr Colbert's I'd seen him, but I see I must have been wrong. I took meals at his house, did I? I don't concern myself with memories. This accusation is unexpected. If I did not know it is an educated man who is making it, I would simply smile, if you will allow me. As it is, I am well aware that I am too stupid to understand how that conclusion was reached.'

'Modlizki! I've lost my livelihood and it's your fault, Modlizki. You hated Laub, but you hated me even more, otherwise you would have brought about my death and not his . . . oh God . . . oh God . . .'

Josef Blau collapsed onto the chair. He hid his face in his hands. Modlizki said nothing. Then Josef Blau heard his voice again.

'I believe I have spoken about all this. I have obviously not been understood. I feel no hatred, I hate no one. Did I not say that? If I felt hatred, I would belong, if that is the right way of putting it. But we do not belong. It's a grand theatre, where the ladies and gentlemen act out their parts, and we are sitting in our seats, in the dark, one beside the other, and we do not move and do not cry and do not laugh, it is as if we did not see or hear it, and I believe that eventually the actors will start to feel uneasy and that will lead to disorder and despair.'

166

'Yes, yes,' said Josef Blau. That was not what he had come for. He would get up and leave. Not return home any more. Leave everything behind him, forget everything, be without guilt, no longer entangled in anything with no way out. He got up. He did not look at Modlizki. He looked out of the window at the green tree-tops. He saw the back of the white goddess. 'Yes, yes,' he said, 'disorder and despair is what has happened to me.'

'I believe I am being done an injustice. I did not have that in mind and I am not to blame for it.'

'Who then? Karpel? He stayed away. He wasn't at school. Why didn't he come himself?'

'I did not have that in mind, I say, and as far as the young gentleman is concerned, that is not the reason why he stayed away from school, he has other matters to concern him. I think everything should go a different way and the world could be different, and I believe it would be good if it were different and that is why I am here. For we are a great mass and they face us, each as a single individual, and things could change if we are recalcitrant but obedient – for we have no power and they would compel us to obey – if we do not smile, do not cry, do not join in and drive them to distraction and despair so that what is our due will come to us, for we are a great mass and strong and without number. That is the reason for it and not hatred. For I can see no other way than the one I go and my example will be seen and followed.'

Modlizki took a step backwards. He spoke more quickly than usual. Josef Blau turned his eyes away from the window and towards him. There were small beads of sweat on Modlizki's brow.

'Forgive me, but there is a reason for saying this. It is not about the picture, but the young gentleman. Master Karpel has fallen into my hands. I have nothing to fear, however it turns out, for I have done nothing but fulfil requests and act as is appropriate for a man of my station. I have no qualms of conscience. The young gentlemen are losing their nerve and their fathers will lose theirs too, but we are here and we have no nerves and no memories of parents, teachers and white statues, and no education, and so nothing will move us if people follow my example. I have not deceived the young gentleman, it is he who did not recognise me for what I was, since he found me obedient and ready to do anything. I was not moved by his goodness and his slim body and his neatly brushed hair, for it was essential I should not be moved by it and I had the strength to resist. For I know what is at stake and why it must happen. If he were to call for me, I would not go. But the young gentleman will not call for me.'

Modlizki went to the window. He leant over the breast and looked out. Josef Blau followed his eye. Between the trees a stretch of the road and a few houses and gardens could be seen.

'That's where it is,' said Modlizki, pointing to a two-storey house a little farther in towards the city. 'The windows are open.'

'What is wrong with him?'

'Nothing yet. If anything had happened it would be obvious. People would gather, Herr Karpel senior would be informed and come home. You would be able to see his car if he was there. It is an American car.'

'What is it, Modlizki? Is he in danger? Oh God, what have you done to him? Don't talk in riddles. You must help him. He might even. . . . No, no, not that again, Modlizki. You must stop it, Modlizki.'

'I do not think that is part of my duties.'

'What is happening? He's going to do away with himself, for God's sake! You know! You can save him. Hurry, hurry before it's too late. You will be to blame for his death, save him, save him!'

'I was the beginning and the companion of everything he did, a man of obscure origins, a servant. I am sure he despises himself for it and my arrival would not save him, even if I wanted to, for it would fill the young gentleman with shame, there is no doubt about that. Even if there is still time, he cannot be brought back from the brink by me.'

'I . . . I . . . Modlizki what are you entangling me in again, oh God . . . I wanted . . . Why did I come to see you . . . No, no, he . . . I can't, Modlizki, it's not my affair, what has it to do with me, it's your affair. It will be on your head, not on mine . . . Jesus, Mary and Joseph . . . say something, tell me it's not true. Why are you standing there saying nothing? All right, I'm going . . . there's nothing else, no, no.' He went up to Modlizki, grasped his arm and squeezed it. 'Oh you . . . why did you tell me? We will not see each other again. I'm not afraid of you any more, you're a fool, a madman and a weakling. Now it's you who are afraid, or whatever you want to call it, rebel against the social order that you are, and you shift it onto others.'

He let go of him and hurried out through the garden. With a buzz the gate clicked open in front of him.

He must not get there too late. He must not, now it was all over, be responsible for Karpel's death as well. He must run, run towards that house there, to the gate, whether he wanted to or not, there was nothing else for it but to stay by Karpel's side until someone came to whom he could entrust the task. He did not have to speak to Karpel, just be there, perhaps he could send for Karpel's father, hand his son into his care, for it was not Josef Blau's affair, only his affair until someone else came, he was only going because there was nothing else for it if he were not to burden himself with guilt, that was why he was running through the front garden, climbing the broad steps and going in through a heavy, carved door. An old servant looked at him in surprise. Josef Blau was breathing heavily, his face was red.

'The young gentleman,' he panted.

'Who should I say is calling?'

'It's urgent.'

He followed the servant over the thick carpets which deadened the sound of their footsteps. They went up a wooden staircase with carved banisters to the second floor. The servant knocked on a door and went in. The door was left ajar. Josef Blau could hear Karpel's voice and the servant's voice replying. There is no time to lose, thought Josef Blau. He pushed the door open and went past the servant into Karpel's room.

Karpel rose. Standing behind a large table covered with books and jotters, he stared at Josef Blau.

The servant stayed by the door, waiting. Without changing his posture, or the direction in which he was looking, Karpel gave him a sign. The servant left, closing the door silently behind him.

The room had two windows. Between them was a glass door, open, leading out onto a balcony. On the walls were coloured engravings in plain frames. A door to the left, which was ajar, led into Karpel's bedroom. In the corner to the left of the windows was a table with cigarettes and ashtrays between two low, cloth-covered armchairs, by the wall opposite a grand piano with the lid open. The walls were hung with a plain dark fabric. The massive rectangular table in the middle was made of dark wood and had no cloth on it. On the side nearest the window was the tall wooden chair Karpel had stood up from when Josef Blau came in. Karpel's eyes were red, as if after a sleepless night. His hair had not been brushed and was hanging down over his eyes. He was wearing a black velvet jacket with braid, only partly done up, and long, wide velvet trousers with a broad black band down the seam.

'I've come from Modlizki,' said Josef Blau.

Karpel's head sank to his chest.

'Sit,' said Josef Blau.

Karpel obeyed.

'Continue with what you were doing, Karpel. I will stay until your father comes.'

Karpel sat slumped in his chair. His head was bowed low over the table. Josef Blau's eye was caught by the colourful cover of a book. It was a description of the conquest of Mexico by Cortez. He sat down opposite Karpel and began to leaf through it. He could hear Karpel's breathing, but Karpel did not raise his head. How long would it be before his father came? It must be about eleven now. Where was there a bell? Perhaps Josef Blau ought to ring, call the servant, raise the alarm. There must be others in the house, Karpel's mother, servants. If Karpel tried to shoot himself, Josef Blau would not be able to take the gun off him by himself. But Karpel was sitting as he did at school, head bowed, unmoving, except that his hair was untidy, like the table with the books, jotters and sheets of paper on it. How long had they been sitting there already? How many times had Josef Blau leafed through the book he was holding in his hands? But now Karpel was raising his head. Josef Blau lowered the book. Karpel leapt up, sending the chair crashing to the floor behind him. Josef Blau stood up too.

'No! No!' Karpel shouted, 'I won't put up with it any more. What are you doing here? I knew you were cruel, but . . . I am no longer your pupil, do you understand? Who gave you permission to come in here uninvited? Go, I tell you, go.'

He raised his arm and pointed to the door. His eyes were fixed on Josef Blau with a menacing look.

'You must permit me to stay, Karpel. You can only remove me by force. I refuse to be entangled in anything any more, do you hear? Not any more. It is connected with particular matters, circumstances which are irrelevant here. I do not want to be to blame any more, even if only partly, as with Laub's death, do you understand? I will hand you over to your father.'

'To blame? What business is it of yours, what I'm going to do? Is it my affair or yours? You have no right to stop me.'

'That may be so. But if someone throws themself into the water and someone else happens to see it and the person drowns because the other did nothing to save them – do you not think the one who happened to be passing would be blamed for the suicide's death?'

'You can't stop anything happening, only delay it.'

'That is the whole point. What happens once your father is here is not my affair any more. But I do not think that someone who has once been saved is that likely to jump back in the river.'

'You . . . you . . . I hate you, I've always hated you. Stop trying to save me! I'm your enemy. Go away from me.' Karpel leant his hands on the table. He bowed his head, his shoulders heaved. 'Oh God, oh God! What do you know of me!'

'I know that you hate me.'

'What do you know of me? You've come to save me, have

you? You could have saved me, yes, you and you alone! It wasn't too late then.' With a sob, he turned aside and stood in the balcony door. He leant his head against the frame. 'I sought you,' he said, without looking at his teacher. 'I followed you in the woods after the outing. I saw you behind a tree, oh, how could I forget! When you were ill I asked Herr Leopold to ask you if I might come and see you . . . You could have saved me, you could have helped me, you knew him, you were his friend.'

Karpel turned round. He wiped his cheeks and eyes with a silk handkerchief.

'Forgive me,' he said. His voice had calmed down. 'I'm behaving like a . . . you'll say I'm a child . . . It is too late for anything. Forgive me and grant me one request: please leave me alone.'

Josef Blau was silent. He looked at the table, at the book he had leafed through. It was lying open at a coloured picture. A lot of armed men had surrounded someone. What could it be? A battle? A murder? So Karpel had been looking for him not because he hated him, but because he needed help, and he had repulsed him, reinforced his hatred, he, the teacher had not seen the child in distress? Whatever the boy had done, Josef Blau should have seen the danger Karpel was in, he should have spoken to him, held out his hand to him, helped him. Oh, perhaps he had learnt in time! However late it was, it might not yet be too late. Now he was here, now he would not repulse him, now he would hold out his hand to him, now he would put things right.

'I will help you,' he said softly.

'Help me! If you only knew . . .' He pressed the handkerchief to his eyes.

'You say you are no longer my pupil. You are right. I am no longer your teacher. I have left the school. You know about the picture . . . the drawing . . . stuck on the blackboard.'

'You've seen the picture? Oh God, oh God! It was Modlizki who . . .'

'I don't want to talk about it, Karpel. You see, I only mentioned it because when I left the school, I thought I would

172

have to . . . that there was nothing left for me apart from what you . . . what Laub . . . and now here I am . . . Don't you see, Karpel, you have nothing to fear from me. If I had had any idea . . . . but I will put things right, tell me what I must do, I want to help you.'

Karpel slowly shook his head. He sat down in the armchair by the window and hid his face in his hands.

'I will call Modlizki. He will have to come, even if I have to force . . .'

'No, no,' said Karpel, 'Nothing can help me . . . If you only knew . . . How can I tell you? I was going to write it down so they would find it, afterwards, but not even that, no one will know apart from him. I am sullied, soiled . . . I shudder at myself . . . keep away from me . . . no, no . . . Leave me . . . I don't want to have to speak, to think any more . . . leave me.'

When he cried and sobbed his voice was a child's voice. No, no, he was not a man. A poor, beaten child seeking deliverance. Modlizki, the rebel against the social order, had driven him, a child with nothing to hold on to, to distraction and despair.

'He should be forced to come and see you,' said Josef Blau. 'But now he is hiding, now he is afraid.'

'Modlizki's not afraid. If he told you, it wasn't because he's afraid, but to save me . . . because he . . . loves me. Did he tell you to try? Can't he understand that I won't . . . no, no . . . Leave me . . . I don't want to have to speak, to think any more . . . Leave me.'

'I went to him and he said to me . . . and when I left . . . no, he did not try to hold me back. Karpel . . .' Josef Blau was standing beside Karpel. He put his hand on his head. Karpel leapt up. He shook off Josef Blau's hand and backed away from him towards the window.

'Don't touch me, no, no, nobody must touch me . . . I'm ashamed . . . oh God!'

'Karpel, don't you believe in anything? I mean . . . don't you believe there is something that makes the laws by which all this happens. Even what has happened to you? Don't laugh. The world is not ruled by madness, but by . . .'

'God?'

'God . . . something . . .'

'You believe?'

Josef Blau nodded.

'In what?'

'In what? Yes, in what?' He paused and looked round, as if he were searching for something. Then he smiled. 'I believe in God, the Father Almighty, Maker of heaven and earth, and in Jesus Christ, his only son, our Lord, who was conceived by the Holy Ghost, suffered under Pontius Pilate, was crucified, dead and buried. He descended into hell. On the third day he rose again from the dead and sitteth on the right hand of God the Father Almighty; from thence he shall come to judge the quick and the dead. I believe in the Holy Ghost, the holy Catholic church, the communion of saints, the forgiveness of sins, the resurrection of the body and the life everlasting. Amen. That is what I learnt at school.' He said it quietly, without emphasis, like a child repeating a lesson.

Karpel looked at him in amazement. Then he shook his head. 'No,' he said. 'No! And even if I did believe in something, it wouldn't help me, it's too late . . . Just because I believed, I couldn't . . . no, no.'

He fell silent. Josef Blau looked out of the window into the garden.

'When I go away from here,' he said quietly, without turning to face Karpel, 'I will not go back home. I have left the school and I am going to leave my child and his mother because . . . it's not so easy to explain . . . I'm telling you this because without it when I left Modlizki I might not have come here to stop you carrying out what you have in mind. For I knew you hated me and I knew the drawing in the classroom could not have been made without you. But I did come. Not for your sake, you understand, for my sake. I did not want to be responsible for anything else that happened because of the things I did or did not do, the effects of which would continue when I was gone . . . You don't understand. How could you understand?! But I am going now, and if you carry out what you have in mind, then I am to blame. For I

174

know that if I had loved you more, loved you as I love my child, I would have found some way of saving you.'

'You would have forced me to go on living. Saved? What kind of life would it be . . . I can't look anyone in the face any more. No, no, if you had loved me, you might perhaps have cried for me, mourned for me, but not stopped me. What would be the point? What is there in store for me from now on?'

'Did I know what was in store for me an hour ago when I thought there was nothing left but to die? Karpel, Karpel, only now do I understand.' He turned to Karpel and raised his hands. 'Oh God, oh God, only now do I see, only now do I understand, this moment has opened my eyes. That is the reason for it all, o Lord, that is the reason! Forgive me, you don't understand how I feel. I too was blind, until now I did not understand the ways, I did not have the faith. Look, it is like a mosaic. We only see the individual coloured tiles, but suddenly, all at once, we see them combine into a picture. We are all pupils, in a great class, and all we can see is the difficulty of the exercise we have to do today, we don't see the overall curriculum. One step follows another, one word another, one day another, but suddenly, when we are visited by grace, oh God . . . for a moment the veil is lifted, we see it as I can see it now – I was in despair, but would I be here to help you, Karpel, if there had not been that drawing on the blackboard, and everything that went before it, your hatred of me, or my hatred of you and because of that the drawing and all the rest, an unending chain of things, a series of moments, at the end of which I am here. Now I know that I will save you, for it has all been leading to this moment, bringing good, bringing grace. For something, not for you perhaps, for a stranger, for a word, a deed, an act of charity, who can say at this moment whether what you have suffered is in your curriculum, one day you will know, tomorrow, tomorrow you will feel as I do standing before you at this moment, full of joy, saved! Whatever has happened to you, it has not happened in vain, to make you stronger or weaker, perhaps, richer or poorer, but with greater insight and clearer vision than you had before.'

He stood facing Karpel and grasped his hand.

'Do not reject my hand now. Do not bow your head, Karpel. Do not let me leave without hope. This moment – I thank you, Karpel, I thank you – was I just confused by everything, was I just confused, or did eternity hover over this poor creature for one brief moment?'

Karpel did not withdraw his hand. He slowly lowered his head until it was resting on Josef Blau's shoulder. He did not answer and he did not hold back the tears that ran down his cheeks and onto the cloth of Josef Blau's coat.

'Cry, cry, tears are a good prayer, my child. Do not hold them back, let them flow, death has no power over someone who can cry. We have made room for it in our hearts, it has tempted us in many forms, we have been put to the test, Karpel, and now I do not fear for you any more, my child. Farewell, Karpel. You do not need me any more.'

He went down the stairs and out of the gate into the street. He hesitated for a moment, as if wavering. Then he hurried back into town, back to Josef Albert, Selma, Herr Leopold, Selma's mother and Uncle Bobek to whom he was bound.

Dedalus European Classics

Dedalus European Classics began in 1984 with D.H. Lawrence's translation of Verga's *Mastro Don Gesualdo*. In addition to rescuing major works of literature from being out of print, the editors' other major aim was to redefine what constituted a 'classic'.

Titles available include:

Little Angel – Andreyev   £4.95
The Red Laugh – Andreyev   £4.95
Séraphita (and other tales) – Balzac   £6.99
The Quest of the Absolute – Balzac   £6.99
The Episodes of Vathek – Beckford   £6.99
The Devil in Love – Cazotte   £5.99
Misericordia – Galdos   £8.99
Spirite – Gautier   £6.99
The Dark Domain – Grabinski   £6.99
The Life of Courage – Grimmelshausen   £6.99
Simplicissimus – Grimmelshausen   £10.99
Tearaway – Grimmelshausen   £6.99
The Cathedral – Huysmans   £7.99
En Route – Huysmans   £7.99
The Oblate – Huysmans   £7.99
Parisian Sketches – Huysmans   £6.99
The Other Side – Kubin   £9.99
The Mystery of the Yellow Room – Leroux   £8.99
The Perfume of the Lady in Black – Leroux   £8.99
The Woman and the Puppet – Louÿs   £6.99
Blanquerna – Lull   £7.95
The Angel of the West Window – Meyrink   £9.99
The Golem – Meyrink   £6.99
The Opal (and other stories) – Meyrink   £7.99
The White Dominican – Meyrink   £6.99
Walpurgisnacht – Meyrink   £6.99

Ideal Commonwealths – More/Bacon et al   £7.95
Smarra & Trilby – Nodier   £6.99
The Late Mattia Pascal – Pirandello   £7.99
The Notebooks of Serafino Gubbio – Pirandello   £7.99
Tales from the Saragossa Manuscript – Potocki   £5.99
Manon Lescaut – Prévost   £7.99
Cousin Basilio – Queiroz   £11.99
The Crime of Father Amaro – Queiroz   £11.99
The Mandarin – Queiroz   £6.99
The Relic – Queiroz   £9.99
The Tragedy of the Street of Flowers – Querioz   £9.99
Baron Munchausen – Raspe   £6.99
The Wandering Jew – Sue   £10.99
The Maimed – Ungar   £6.99
The Class – Ungar   £7.99
I Malavoglia (The House by the Medlar Tree) –
   Verga   £7.99
Mastro Don Gesualdo – Verga   £7.99
Short Sicilian Novels – Verga   £ 6.99
Sparrow, Temptation & Cavalleria Rusticana –
   Verga   £8.99
Micromegas – Voltaire   £4.95

The Maimed – Hermann Ungar

'a sexual hell, full of filth, crime and the deepest melancholy –
a monomanical digression, if you will, but nevertheless the
digression of an inwardly pure artistry . . . a masterpiece that
would be honoured in any classic oeuvre.'
   Thomas Mann

'What is with these Czechs? It is not just Kafka: they all seem
to be obsessed with the idea of forces acting against them,
forces of motiveless malevolence. Franz Polzer is that quintes-
sentially 1920s creation, the tormented bank clerk. His outer
life is pristine, his inner one deeply unhygienic: fears of disorder plague him and when his landlady, Frau Polger, begins
to make unmistakably sexual advances to him, his mind
buckles into a state of helpless paranoia. Nor is that all: his best
friend, Karl Fanta, is dying slowly of a hideous wasting disease
which unsettles his reason. Everyone is drowning in a desper-
ate search for security. The destinies of Franz, his landlady,
Karl and a mysterious male nurse converge in a denouement
of madness and murder. Somewhere Polzer knows that whatever it is, it's not his fault, but he can never find the words: the
text seems to hint that a sense of guilt is preferable to bewil-
derment. Polzer himself is a profoundly poignant figure:
one of the novel's most moving moments has Frau Polger
throw out the picture of St Francis which Polzer had always
treasured: "It's just that he was always on the wall above my
bed".'
   Murrough O'Brien in *The Independent on Sunday*

'First English translation of a bleak 1928 novel by a forgotten
Czech member of the generation of Doblin, Brecht and
Werfel. It's a closely concentrated analysis of the frail psyche
of obscure bank clerk Franz Polzer, a timid paranoid whose
obsessive pursuit of order and control lead ironically to helpless explosions of irrationality and violence, and to his even-
tual undoing. Ungar's understated prose (perfectly captured
by veteran translator Mitchell) trains a cold clinical eye on the

processes through which Polzer – in effect, a country mouse adrift in a wicked city – is seduced by his promiscuous landlady and misled by his satanic "best friend," a moribund, wheelchair-bound misanthrope, thus set on a path toward self-destruction. Unusual and unsettling: what a film it would make.'

Kirkus Reviews

'It is a mystery why Hermann Ungar's remarkable novel *The Maimed* has taken seventy years to find an English translation. A French version was published in 1928, five years after the German original, and Ungar's works were admired by many, including Thomas Mann and Stefan Zweig, who described the book as 'Great and terrible, alluring and repulsive – unforgettable, although one would like to forget it and flee the evil sense of oppression it creates.' Ungar, a German-speaking Czech Jew, born in Moravia was often spoken of in the same breath as Kafka.

Despite its grimness, there is also a darkly comic element throughout the book. Ungar's economy of style maintains tension and pace, while the lack of writerly description increases the drama. The writing has a crisp modern edge which the translator Mike Mitchell renders into convincing and natural English.'

Will Stone in *The Times Literary Supplement*

'It is an oddly absorbing and sometimes grotesque tale of Franz Polzer, a classic Kafkaesque everyman, his life governed by the ritual that he has established and yet haunted by the disruption of that order by his demanding landlady. Inevitably, he succumbs and plummets into self degradation that can only end in a death, but the question that must be posed is whose death is it to be? This sobering account of one man's descent from irrational paranoia to self destruction is at once repulsive and captivating.'

Buzz Magazine

£6.99   ISBN 1 903517 10 9   210p   B.Format